ACAPULCO G.P.O.
By Day Keene

Black Gat Books • Eureka California

ACAPULCO G.P.O.

Published by Black Gat Books
A division of Stark House Press
1315 H Street
Eureka, CA 95501, USA
griffinskye3@sbcglobal.net
www.starkhousepress.com

ACAPULCO G.P.O.
Originally published in paperback by Dell Books, New York,
and copyright © 1967 by Day Keene.

Reprinted by permission of Day James, executor of the estate
of Day Keene. All rights reserved under International and Pan-
American Copyright Conventions.

ISBN: 979-8-88601-063-3

Text design by Mark Shepard, shepgraphics.com
Cover design by Jeff Vorzimmer, ¡caliente!design, Austin, Texas
Cover art by Abbett

PUBLISHER'S NOTE:
This is a work of fiction. Names, characters, places and
incidents are either the products of the author's imagination or
used fictionally, and any resemblance to actual persons, living
or dead, events or locales, is entirely coincidental.
Without limiting the rights under copyright reserved above, no
part of this publication may be reproduced, stored, or
introduced into a retrieval system or transmitted in any form
or by any means (electronic, mechanical, photocopying,
recording or otherwise) without the prior written permission of
both the copyright owner and the above publisher of the book.

First Stark House Press/Black Gat Edition: October 2023

"The noir world of his crime novels is populated by misfits, frauds, femmes fatales and predators, their fates played out in fast-paced, darkly humorous narratives: Keene was, as Geoffrey O'Brien says in *Hardboiled America*, 'one of the most adroit plot-spinners of the paperback era.'"—Lee Horsley

"Day Keene is one of the most popular authors here at Paperback Warrior for a reason. His storytelling is masterful and his characters skirt the fine line between moral and immoral."—*Paperback Warrior*

"Day Keene novels are page turners, they bite early and hold firm."—Paul Burke, *Crime Time*

ACAPULCO G.P.O.

"Centered around Acapulco and a nearby former fishing village that's now home to a number of wealthy jet-setters, Keene spins a yarn with a large cast and a number of intersecting storylines… As for plotlines, you get drug smuggling, prostitution, kidnapping, murder, and lots of sex to go along with the crime and violence."
—James Reasoner, *Rough Edges*

BOOK ONE

An azure bay rimmed by palm-clustered hills ... this is Acapulco, your gay exciting playground for fun-filled days. You'll laze on the white-gold beaches of Los Hornos, swim in the sun-warmed water of Caleta. Quaint byways invite leisurely strolls. Colorful shops invite the bargain hunter. Then a romantic tropical sunset brings promise of new thrills.

Chapter One

The Administrador de Correos in Acapulco is as efficient as any high-ranking postal official in Mexico. Despite the facts that during the last two decades Acapulco's permanent population has quadrupled and that the five or six large resort hotels that existed at the end of World War II have burgeoned into three hundred registered hostelries capable of accommodating a million and a half tourists a year, he could make any number of arrangements to have their mail delivered more promptly to the householders, most of them non-nationals, of the two-year-old, sixty-unit, complex built in the wooded foothills of the Sierra Madre del Sur overlooking Paraíso Bay.

Their mail could be despatched on the daily eight-A.M. bus to Zihuatanejo and dropped off at the small copra settlement of Coyuca de Benitez to be distributed from there. It could be delivered by jeep via the twenty-five miles of dusty road that winds along the ocean to a dead end at the tiny shark-fishing village of La Barra de Coyuca.

However, for reasons known only to themselves, most of the residents of the expatriate seaside development built far enough up the coast from Acapulco to escape the high land-value area, but within easy commuting distance by car or small boat, are content to have their correspondence addressed to Rancho Paraíso, in care of General Delivery, Administratión de Correos, Acapulco. There it is sacked and held, and twice a week, on the days when he drives in for supplies or to spend a night with his family, it is picked up and distributed by Señor Miguel Jesus Eduardo Córdoba, who leases and runs the bar and dining-room concession in the once swank private yacht club out of which the development was born.

Hoy. Ayer. Mañana. What difference did a few days make? Living as most of them did on substantial pensions, or on money sent out of their countries ahead of their own hasty departures, time was no longer of the essence to the majority of the people living at Rancho Paraíso. One of the exceptions was Jim Harris, the artist. Time had meaning for him. He had a living to make.

Harris slept fitfully, then awakened with a start shortly after dawn. His head ached. His mouth was dry. When he ran his big hands down his heavily muscled torso he found it covered with a film of perspiration.

He lay for a few minutes with his eyes closed, attempting to orient his thoughts as he listened to the pound of the rollers on the beach, a quarter of a mile away.

There was so much he didn't know, might never know. He did know two things. One, if the powers that were wanted to be consistent in their concern for the general weal, along with insisting that all cigarettes manufactured in the Estados Unidos de la America del Norte had to bear the notation—"Caution: Cigarette Smoking May Be Hazardous To Your Health"—every male child that was born should be compelled to have his male member tattooed with the legend—"Warning: Extended Adult Use May Lead To Serious Physical and Mental Complications."

He also knew he was drinking too heavily. Both he and Sonia were. From what he remembered of their most recent quarrel it had been particularly acrimonious, with both of them shouting the standard accusations and denials.

Being careful not to awaken the wife sleeping beside him, Harris felt for his cigarettes and lit one. Their marriage had been a mistake. He could see that now. Few artists married their models. A man painted the girl as he saw her. Then he did one of two things. He paid her the agreed upon fee and sent her on her way. Or, if the physical attraction was mutual and strong, he had an affair with the girl that lasted until both parties were satiated and ready to move on to a fresh canvas.

He pursued this line of thought. During his student days in Paris, and in the years before he'd become engrossed in murals and portraiture, he'd painted a hundred nudes and gone to bed with a third of them. There was nothing new or abnormal about that. What was abnormal was the fact that five years after they'd first met, he and Sonia were still married. He was washed up professionally and emotionally at thirty-five. Sonia was still young and vital enough to be in demand as a model by every hack artist south of the border dedicated to calendar art or slightly pornographic life-size playroom nudes. But they stayed married.

Harris tried to be honest with himself as he chewed on the cotton in his mouth. It wasn't Sonia posing in the nude for other men that bothered him. It was the fact that she felt compelled to use her body to earn money because he could no longer make a decent living for them with his brushes. It made him feel like a pimp. Maybe he was.

He turned his head on the pillow and studied Sonia's face. Sonia was Viennese, and she had a Continental attitude toward sex. She liked it. Any way. Any place. Any time. On the other hand she flatly denied any breach of the marital code. Sometime during their quarrel last night she had said:

"Look, Jim. Be reasonable. We're up to our necks in debt. Everything we have is in this house. And if we hope to keep it one of us must earn enough to make the payments and meet the other bills. The mere fact that I've returned to modeling is no reason for you to suspect me of being unfaithful with every artist I pose for. I wasn't a virgin when I came to you. I never pretended to be. But no other man has possessed me since I first gave myself to you. I swear it, Jim."

Harris continued to study Sonia's sleeping face. She'd said it all in the quaint accent that was so much a part of her. That much he remembered. He'd been so convinced of her sincerity that he'd swept her up in his arms and carried her into the bedroom. For the time it had taken them to undress everything had been as it had always been with them. And then, just when he'd been about to take her, just when Sonia was smiling up at him with her soft white thighs splayed to receive him, it had happened— again.

He was impotent.

A car passed on the road leading down to the bay. From the sound of the motor he knew it was Señor Córdoba's jeep. Harris eased himself out of bed, stood for a moment looking down at his wife, then stooped and brushed her honey colored hair with his lips.

God knew he didn't want it to be this way. It was driving him out of what little mind he had left. He took his robe from the back of a chair and walked down the hall to the kitchen, wondering if he was completely sane. After last night's failure, naturally, he'd ... no, he really didn't know what he'd done. The last thing he remembered was being back in the living room sucking on an almost empty bottle of bourbon, impelled by an overwhelming desire to strike out at something, anything.

He filled the tea kettle with water and put it on the stove. Then he went into the living room and explored the liquor cabinet.

Either he or Sonia had finished the bourbon. That left vermouth or tequila. Harris uncorked the tequila bottle. At least he had one thing for which to be grateful. Now that the international set had discovered Acapulco, and prices had risen accordingly, tequila offered one of the few remaining avenues of escape that didn't cost too much.

He drank from the bottle. Then, realizing the kettle was whistling, he carried the bottle into the kitchen, heaped several spoonfuls of instant coffee into a beer mug and filled the mug with boiling water.

It wasn't as good as percolator coffee but it was hot and strong. He sweetened it with tequila, carried the mug and the bottle out onto the flagged front patio, and sat at the small metal table under the flowering jacaranda tree. He watched as Señor Córdoba, assisted by Pepe and Juan, began to unload the supplies that

Córdoba had purchased on his semi-weekly trip into town.

A few puddles of rain lay on the flagging but the onshore wind had died and even this early the air was pleasantly warm. The cheeping of the birds in the branches over his head and the boom of the foam-flecked surf insisted that he must somehow contrive to live on and enjoy a truly beautiful morning.

The usual complement of pelicans, ibises, egrets and herons were wheeling above the placid surface of the lagoon or feeding in the shallows. Beyond the rope suspension bridge separating the lagoon from the rougher boat basin, the various small boats and cabin cruisers and the two-place seaplane belonging to Cara Lane's latest boy friend lay at anchor. With the clubhouse and homes scattered through the hills, the scene was much as it had been when Hernando Cortés, the famous Captain of Castile, had despatched three caravels from Acapulco in search of the legendary Seven Cities of Cibola.

Harris sighed. The only thing he'd done right in the last two years had been to buy a house in Rancho Paraíso. Making the stiff down payment and furnishing the house had taken all his ready cash and what money he could borrow. But if he could hold on to the house until the real-estate boom spread this far up the coast, he should easily triple or quadruple his investment.

He appraised what he could see of the development. Erected on natural pads in the wooded foothills rimming the coast, with ample ground around them to insure privacy, the units in the complex had been conceived by creative architects and built by artisans who knew their business. No two houses were alike but all had red Spanish tile roofs, two or more bedrooms, a family or rumpus room, ultramodern baths and kitchens and enormous living rooms with exposed-beam ceilings, floor-to-ceiling fireplaces of natural stone and wide glass doors which slid open onto the flagged and landscaped patios that overlooked the clubhouse, the communal swimming pool and the bay.

North of the border a similar home would cost four times more.

Harris added another dollop of tequila to the coffee left in the mug. He couldn't say as much for his neighbors as he could for their houses. In a sense, living at Rancho Paraíso was like inhabiting a Lautrec lithograph full of Moulin Rouge characters. They ranged from unusual to grotesque, and they were all originals.

General Ti and Cara Lane were good examples.

The big, soft-spoken Chinese was supposed to have been a prominent general in the People's Army of China before he'd defected to Hong Kong with a large helping of the People's money. Some residents of the enclave insisted that Ti's break with the party was final and that he had a price on his head. Others maintained that his alleged defection was a cover. They said his current mission was directing the rapidly expanding, illicit drug trade that reputedly financed a large part of Red China's military budget and sudden progress in other fields.

Harris lit a cigarette and inhaled. All he knew for sure about General Ti was that he maintained a small import and export business in Acapulco, shot golf in the low eighties, had a White Russian wife who played an excellent game of bridge, and idolized his sixteen-year-old daughter, Lotus, who for some reason was known as Sally to the other teenagers in the enclave.

There was no mystery about Cara Lane's reason for living in Mexico. The still beautiful American motion-picture star and one time box-office attraction, having barely escaped being indicted for the still unsolved but not so mysterious murder of her then current lover in her Malibu Beach home, had been black-listed by every major studio in the States and was attempting to make a place for herself in the Spanish-speaking movie community.

Harris had no feeling, one way or another, about Cara Lane. If she wanted to shoot her lover because she caught him with another woman, that was her business. He did feel sorry for Tasy, the green-eyed and rather plain-faced teenager with red hair who was the result of one of her mother's youthful amatory efforts.

Ti and Cara Lane were only two of many. Other residents of importance included one former head of state and one deposed premier who had negotiated Khyber Pass two camels ahead of a firing squad.

Belonging to these personages was a small horde of offspring who lived in their swim trunks and bikinis and who, when they weren't surfboarding or water-skiing or running the road to Acapulco, seemed to spend their days dropping coins in the clubhouse jukebox and shaking their private parts at each other and, for all Harris knew, their nights trying to find new ways to fit them together.

Harris made a fist and pounded the metal table softly. He'd better think about his own faults. He'd thought things had been as bad as they could get until this latest development. For no apparent reason, he'd just suddenly stopped selling. He hadn't had a decent commission in over a year. Except for the money Sonia made by allowing hacks like Abdul Ahmed to immortalize her beautiful derriere in oil, their only income was from what little money he earned by painting quick bargain-price portraits from colored snapshots sent him by readers of the advertisements he'd placed in several of the lesser monthly publications in the United States:

> HAVE THE CELEBRATED SOCIETY ARTIST JAMES HARRIS PAINT YOUR LOVED ONE'S PORTRAIT FROM YOUR FAVORITE COLORED SNAPSHOT. $75 to $250 DEPENDING ON THE SIZE OF PORTRAIT CHOSEN....

He also earned a few dollars by giving art lessons to a dozen teenage residents of the community who considered studying art just another way of killing time but whose doting parents were under the impression they'd conceived present-day Rosa Bonheurs.

The supplies had long since been unloaded from the jeep and Harris watched, mildly interested, as Señor Córdoba, obviously excited, came out of the recreation lounge adjoining the combination bar and dining room waving several yellow objects and a white one at his helpers. At that distance, it was difficult to determine what he was displaying but from where Harris sat it looked as if the portly Mexican concessionaire had come up with a pair of discarded yellow capri pants, a matching halter and a pair of briefs.

Harris smiled grimly as he rose to his feet. How was it the poet had put it? Oh, yes. "You never miss the violets until they're gone."

He walked into the house to put on a pair of slacks

and some sandals. There might be a couple of orders in the new sack of mail. At the same time he could find out why Córdoba was so excited.

He hoped Sonia would still be asleep. She wasn't. She was sitting on the edge of the bed holding her head in her hands. As he entered the room she peered at him through her spread fingers.

"My God, Jim. How much did I drink last night?"

"We both drank plenty," Harris said.

"Are you as hung over as I am?"

"I was. But I just had a cup of black coffee spiked with tequila and it helped."

"Then I'd better try some," Sonia said. She took her hands away from her face and watched him as he discarded his robe and took a clean pair of slacks from the closet. "Where are you going this time of morning?"

Harris felt his cheeks growing hot under her scrutiny. "Down to the clubhouse."

"Again?"

"What do you mean, again?"

"You don't remember?"

Harris continued to be embarrassed as he struggled into and zipped up his slacks. "Remember what?"

"Storming out of here about two o'clock this morning?"

"No."

"Well, you did." Sonia stood up and came toward him.

"After accusing me of everything in the book."

Harris tried not to look at her nude body. "I'm sorry."

"You should be," Sonia said quietly. "You said terrible things to me, Jim. You went away, and then you came back half an hour later, soaking wet, as if you'd fallen into the pool. You got back into bed and I snuggled up to you and said I was sorry. I wanted to prove how much I love you. I said so. And what did you do?"

It was an effort for Harris to ask. "All right. I'll bite. What did I do?"

Still standing nude in front of him, Sonia shook her head gently.

"Nothing. Absolutely nothing." Her lower lip quivered. "Who is she, Jim?"

Harris blinked. "Who is who?"

"The girl you're sleeping with," Sonia said. "The one you spend so much time making love to that you have nothing left for me."

Chapter Two

Sonia's dull headache, localized in her temples now, persisted as she sat at the table in the kitchen, dawdling over her third cup of black coffee and staring through the open window at the flurry of activity on the far side of the pool.

It was all very puzzling. Jim had walked down the road to the clubhouse, disappeared into the lounge, and then emerged a few seconds later with Señor Córdoba. After an earnest conversation, Señor Córdoba had said something to Pepe and Pepe had jumped into the jeep and driven at breakneck speed up the road leading to the Ti house. A few minutes later, General and Mrs. Ti had arrived with Pepe and they all had disappeared into the lounge.

Now a dozen other couples, arriving on foot and by car, including Dr. and Marcia Wilder and the Brunos and Colonel and Mrs. Amapa, were standing in tight little clusters on the flagging just outside the door of the club, peering into the lounge from time to time as they conversed as earnestly as Jim and Señor Córdoba had. Neither Mr. nor Mrs. Carlson was in the crowd but Andy, their nineteen-year-old son, was there with Tasy Lane and Brunnhilde and the Anderson girl along with half a dozen other teenagers.

Sonia wondered where Sally was. Usually the pretty little Eurasian and Tasy and Brunnhilde were inseparable. The Unholy Three, Jim called them. What one couldn't think of, the others could.

She returned her attention to young Carlson. Many Swedish males were very handsome. Young Carlson was one of them. Almost as tall as Jim, with spectacularly blond hair he looked like a travel-poster Viking. Besides, he was so rich. Not only did his expatriate father own a large travel agency in Acapulco, with branches in Bogotá and Buenos Aires, but according to the last issue in *La Verdad,* Carlson senior had been granted Mexican citizenship and had purchased a majority interest in a new deluxe hotel on Hotel Row.

Sonia poured fresh coffee in her cup. It would be nice to have so much money. For the first few years of her marriage to Jim she'd thought that was the way it was going to be for them. He hadn't been able to paint fast enough to turn out the high-priced portraits that people wanted. Five thousand, ten thousand dollars for each commission, and both of them spending the money as fast as it had come in. Suddenly, for no reason at all, a little over a year ago, the orders had stopped coming. As if someone had drawn a curtain.

It happened that way to artists, Elsie had told her, especially to artists whose work was highly specialized as Jim's was. But Elsie had also told her that when artists were as talented as Jim was, their dry periods seldom lasted long. "Do what you can to keep him painting," Elsie had said. "Hold on to what you've saved. He'll come back into vogue again."

That was why, in spite of his objections, Sonia had insisted on returning to figure work. What difference did it make? Her return to modeling was merely a means to an end. She didn't care how famous an artist was. Given some measure of security, she wouldn't pose nude again if Gauguin came back to life and insisted on painting her with a red hibiscus over one ear and a bluebird perched on one nipple.

Sonia opened her peignoir and looked first at her breasts, then down between them at the crisp, flat, honey-colored triangle between her thighs. "Jim doesn't love us anymore," she told them sadly. "The not so little gentleman has found a new home."

Sullen-eyed, she closed the negligee. She didn't know what to do. But she did know she would never be poor, really poor, again. She didn't intend to go through that business a second time. Once had been quite sufficient.

She looked back at the growing crowd in front of the clubhouse. How many of them knew what it was like to be really poor?

To be poor, as she'd been poor, they would have to dispose of everything they owned—clothing, houses, cars— and move into an unheated storage loft over a bombed-out shop on the Schönlaterngasse owned by a slightly crazy old countess who was trying to eke out her few remaining years by selling the few possessions the Allied bombers had left her.

Sonia compromised. Oh, yes. She would let those people keep one hot plate, one old-fashioned *Wasserklosett* with a long chain, a yellow-stained washbasin, and one huge black-marble bathtub large enough for Archduke Francis Ferdinand and his consort to play house in.

She started to spoon sugar into the coffee and was struck by a sudden thought. Now that Acapulco had become an international resort, one of the men who had known and possessed her in Vienna might have recognized her, and told Jim. That could be it. She spilled the sugar on the table.

She should have insisted on telling Jim about the bad days before she agreed to marry him. But during their first days together, every time she'd tried to talk about Vienna he'd stoppered her mouth with a kiss.

In the end, she hadn't told him anything, not even about Steve Melancz.

Sonia spat through the open window beside her. That for Sergeant Stephen Arpad Melancz. But it hadn't been entirely Steve's fault. Finding her where he had, doing what she'd been doing when they'd met, she supposed he'd had every right to believe she would be content with the life he'd offered her.

Sonia realized her breathing had become labored. The hot morning Mexican sun seemed suddenly less bright. It was no longer so warm in the kitchen that even her thin white peignoir was superfluous. Nor was she any longer stationary, sitting at her own table, in her own kitchen. As in the worst of her dreams, she was back riding the ancient Riesenrad in the Prater, with the two-hundred-and-ten-foot high Ferris wheel out of control while a nearby phonograph played the haunting "Third Man" melody as recorded on a scratched record.

Vienna
November 24, 1954

"Yes, of course, Frau von Erlac," the harassed but very proper British lieutenant said. "We understand your concern. But these things take time. If your husband was arrested by the Russians, it may be weeks, even months before we can establish a contact."

Sitting on the edge of the straight chair beside his desk, Sonia started to remind him that two months had passed since the Russians had knocked on their door in the middle of the night and taken Eric away. She refrained. She'd told him that. She'd told it to every officer, British, French and American, who would listen to her. The lieutenant meant well. And all he could do was send her request back through the regular channels.

"I'll tell you what," Lieutenant Eden said. "Leave your new address with me. And as soon as we learn anything definite, I'll contact you."

"Whatever you say," Sonia said.

She wrote her name, including her given and maiden names, so there couldn't be any mistake, and her new address on the printed form the lieutenant laid in front of her.

"Sonia, eh?" the lieutenant said. "That's a Russian name, isn't it?"

"So I am told." Sonia smiled. "It would seem that one of my male ancestors married a Russian woman."

After she completed the form she bade the officer *Guten Abend* and stood up and made her way through the maze of desks to the door. Out in the deepening night and the cold, Sonia buttoned her thin spring coat against the cold wind blowing off the Danube and paused for a moment, envying two warmly dressed British sergeants who were checking the uniforms and pistols and other gear of a four-man international patrol. The patrol consisted of a Russian, a French, a British and an American M.P., and the four men were about to start on a cruise of the city in one of their high-powered reconnaissance cars.

She walked on with the wind whipping her skirt so high, at times, that she had to reach down and hold it in place to keep from being immodest. The least Frau and Herr Krueger could have done was to allow her to take one pair of warm pants before they locked her out of her apartment.

She considered her marriage to Eric as she walked past the gutted skeleton of a bombed-out building. Some aspects of her marriage had been mildly pleasant. She'd enjoyed cooking and keeping house and bargaining with shopkeepers. She'd tried to be a good wife. But now, try as hard as she could, she was unable to feel any great sense of personal bereavement.

Perhaps she had been too young to grasp the full significance of marriage. Not once during the year they'd lived together as man and wife had Eric ever completely awakened her. She'd always felt she was on the verge of a great and beautiful discovery but nothing truly dramatic had ever happened. Eric had been so afraid he might impregnate her, afraid he'd have a third mouth to feed on his twenty-eight-dollar a month translator's pay. So he'd always insisted on "protecting" her. She giggled hysterically, then forced herself to be calm.

Never mind all that. Eric was gone, and because she hadn't been able to pay the two months' rent due on their apartment, the Kruegers had locked her out. She'd been forced to spend her last few schillings to rent the cubicle in the loft over Frau Voelker's antique shop.

Sonia supposed she should feel bitter. She did. On the other hand, this was her first really bad experience with the war. Both Trudi and Hilda had told her wild tales about the early days, but she'd just been born when the Germans had marched into Austria and still much too young to be personally concerned when the "liberating" Russians had arrived. All she knew was that since she was five years old, she and her mother had moved constantly and each new house or apartment had been a little smaller and shabbier than the previous one.

Sonia walked on blindly through the cold, attempting to ignore the good things that were beginning to appear in the shop windows and the savory smells issuing from the coffee houses and sidewalk cafés catering mainly to the occupation forces and the tourists.

She knew one way to survive. Hundreds of girls in Vienna, girls from good families, were selling themselves in order to eat and pay their rent. She might come to that.

"You're foolish not to," Trudi had told her. "With that figure of yours you could make a fortune. You could ask for at least forty schillings."

Sonia realized that by walking blindly she'd wound up on the Ringstrasse. She hurried on, eager to regain the dubious comfort of her newly rented cubicle over Frau Voelker's shop.

She was so cold that her teeth chattered as she hurried past a sign-plastered kiosk. A youthful American G.I., well bundled against the cold in a heavy O.D. greatcoat and a fur cap, was idly tossing a small object in the palm of one gloved hand as he leaned against a torn poster of a white dove in a cage bearing the legend: "No Peace without Freedom."

As she passed him he asked casually, "How about it, Fraulein? Want to make my last night in Vienna a beautiful memory?"

Sonia turned to make an angry retort, then realized

that the object he was tossing in his palm was a small bar of soap in its original wrapper. He was clean-shaven, young, possibly twenty-two or twenty-three. He radiated an aura of well-scrubbed cleanliness. His last night in Vienna, eh? If he was telling the truth she wouldn't ever have to see him again.

She tried to walk on and couldn't. Instead, she heard herself saying, almost without volition, "Well, I'll tell you what, soldier. Instead of standing here in the cold, why don't we go somewhere and have a glass of wine and a bit to eat? Perhaps we can work out something."

"Good," the soldier said. He pushed himself away from the wall of the kiosk and gripped her elbow. "I'm Pfc Jerry Lansing. What do they call you, honey?"

Sonia could feel her knees giving under her as they climbed the outside stairs, but she managed to unlock and open the door, then turn on the unshaded light bulb and start the gas heater at the foot of the bed.

"You don't have much of a place here, do you?" Pfc Lansing said.

"No," Sonia admitted, "I don't."

She hung her thin coat on a nail. Her new friend removed his fur cap and greatcoat, plunged his hand into his pants pocket, and laid forty schillings and the small bar of soap on the battered chest of drawers.

She felt slightly lightheaded from the wine she'd drunk and suddenly embarrassed, not quite knowing what to do next.

Her guest solved her problem. He sat on the edge of the sagging double bed, pulling her down on his lap and kissing her. Than he ran one of his hands up under her skirt.

"Nice. Very nice, Fraulein," he said. "Now, how about letting me undress you?"

Sonia stood up. She allowed him to pull her dress over her head, unhook her brassiere and slip her thin panties down over her hips, pausing from time to time to admire and kiss and fondle what he exposed. Then, when she was completely nude, he told her to get into bed. A minute later he joined her.

His lovemaking was expert, possessive. Unlike Eric, he made no attempt to "protect" her. Then with their bodies still joined and his sticky male juices cementing their newly formed friendship, Sonia allowed him to turn her on her side. They lay facing each other, and he brushed her lips with his.

"That was wonderful, simply wonderful, baby. That was out of this world. But now we know each other a little better, tell me. How come a good-looking girl like you, you know, stacked the way you are and everything, how come you're willing to put out for a meal and a few drinks? I mean even with the Austrian schilling holding fairly steady at twenty-seven for a dollar, it only amounts to around a lousy buck sixty cents."

Pfc Lansing was shocked and angry when she told him about Eric. He was more shocked and sympathetic when she told him about the Kruegers locking her out of her apartment. And it was a fact that, until he'd taken her to the café, all she'd had to eat for four days had been several bowls of barley and lentil soup and a piece of *Sachertorte* which one of her girl friends had given her.

Now, as she lay alone in the disordered but snug cocoon formed by the quilt and Pfc Lansing's coat, listening to his booted feet clomp down the outside stairs and merge with the night silence of the Schönlaterngasse, Sonia reflected smugly that while he'd been very sympathetic, Pfc Lansing had nevertheless invaded her helpless body twice more before he'd kissed her *auf Wiedersehen* and gone off to catch his plane.

When she could no longer hear his footsteps she crawled out of her cocoon. Ignoring the bitter cold that the gas heater failed to dispel, she sat nude on the edge of the rumpled bed and smoked a cigarette from the full package of Camels he'd left her.

She wished she had a mirror. She knew her hair was untidy. Her makeup was probably a mess. There were matters that needed urgent attention and she had only cold water with which to attend herself.

She supposed she should feel ashamed of herself. But she didn't. After a dreary year of marriage to an enfeebled old man she'd found out what it was like to make love with a young, virile, amply endowed partner.

She sucked at her cigarette thoughtfully. True, the first time Lansing had possessed her nothing unusual had happened. She'd still been too embarrassed to respond to him. All it had been was pleasant.

Sonia filled her lungs with smoke and exhaled harshly. But the second and third time—*Ach Gott!* Both times her fiercely upthrust body had literally forced him to rush panting to his final satisfaction, and her own prolonged and ecstatic reaction had been almost more than she could bear. She'd had all she could do to keep from screaming.

Sonia looked down through a veil of smoke at the pale triangle ornamenting the juncture of her thighs. *Jawohl,* She'd done her best to please Pfc Jerry Lansing, and he— Well, he had not only opened an entire new world to her, he had insisted on proving his gratitude.

First he had given her his greatcoat and fur cap.

"You need them more than I do, kid," he'd told her. "Besides, that's what supply sergeants are for." Then, after he'd buttoned his tunic, reluctantly, he'd plunged his hand into his pants pocket again and without bothering to count it had rained a shower of paper and silver money on top of the forty schillings and the bar of soap.

"And you might as well have this, too. What the hell, it's only money."

Sonia took the fur cap from the bed post and cocked it on her head at a jaunty angle, then counted the money on the chest of drawers. It was true then: all *Amerikaners* were millionaires. Including the forty schillings, Pfc Lansing had left her twenty-six dollars and eighty cents. Sonia was awed. It was almost as much as Eric had earned in a month and it had taken her less than three hours to earn it.

She'd been expecting a knock on the door. When it came she called, "Come in."

Frau Voelker's stringy gray hair was done up in paper curlers. One of her gnarled, age-spotted hands clutched the frayed edges of a long, outmoded heavy flannel dressing gown over her ancient and sagging paps. She was so angry she could hardly speak.

"I heard," she spluttered. "I heard. Now you get out of my house, you naked little rip. Right now. *Seien Sie schnell.* I didn't rent this room to—"

"I know," Sonia said. "You didn't rent me this room to entertain men. You are a very good and deeply religious woman and you won't have me bringing shame on your establishment." She draped the army coat around her bare shoulders in lieu of a dressing gown and stood up. "But now let me tell you something, Frau Voelker. I have no intention of moving. I suddenly like it right where I am."

Frau Voelker continued to sputter. Sonia picked up a handful of bills, counted rapidly and thrust the money into the old woman's hands. "So there is a month's rent in advance," she said. "There will be an additional five dollars every week if you'll see to it that there is always hot water." She added, pointedly, "Enough hot water for bathing and for whatever other purpose may be needed. *Heute Abend.*"

Greed and need replaced the landlady's anger as she fingered the bills. For a moment Sonia thought she was going to curtsey. Instead, she stuffed the money into the front of her robe and scuttled to the door.

"Jawohl. It shall be as you wish, Frau von Erlac. I will go and light the heater right away."

"And I want a mirror over the chest of drawers and a key for the inner door and another pillow," Sonia called after her.

"Jawohl. Whatever you say, Frau von Erlac."

Sonia sat down on the bed and unwrapped the bar of soap. Holding it in one hand, she listened to the rumbling in the ancient water pipes. From time to time she got up to test the hot-water tap in the massive black-marble bathtub. Finally the water ran hot enough to suit her. She shrugged off the heavy coat. Still wearing the fur cap, she half-filled the tub and climbed in. After she splashed water on herself she soaped her body generously, paying particular attention to the portion that had held the most appeal for the departed G.I. She hoped he hadn't impregnated her. But it was just one of the chances she would have to take, now that she had become a public woman.

For the next six months Sonia was the belle of the *Schönlaterngasse,* the Lili Marlene of the Ringstrasse. A long parade of American, British and French enlisted men and officers followed her up the outside stairs of Frau Voelker's antique shop.

Sometime during that period the very proper Lieutenant Eden of Allied High Command had dropped in late one Sunday afternoon. He had come to inform her that she was now the youthful widow von Erlac; they now knew definitely that Eric had been a double agent and had been executed somewhere in the Russian sector. And then Lieutenant Eden had tarried to "console" Sonia, and add a few British pounds to her growing collection of francs and schillings and American dollars.

On occasions, when she felt unaccountably depressed, Sonia tried to total the number of men with whom she had stayed, but couldn't. She couldn't even remember most of their faces. At the time, all that mattered was that they were male and rigidly amorous and willing to pay to use her body as an animated receptacle into which to vent their passion.

Ten years later and half a world away, Sonia von Erlac Harris spooned sugar into her coffee and reflected somberly that even now, every time a strange man stared at her, she wondered, *Did I ever with him? How many times? What if he tells Jim?*

Sonia sipped the cold coffee. It could be that one of her former "clients" had recognized and told Jim the whole filthy business. If not that, then he must be having an affair with some girl or woman in the enclave. It had to be one or the other. He certainly didn't want or need her any more.

She pursued this line of thought. But if Jim knew, why didn't he say something? Why didn't he slap her, beat her, call her a dirty whore. If he wanted her to she'd crawl, beg him to forgive her for deceiving him.

She'd do whatever he wanted her to do as long as he didn't stop loving her.

This business of claiming to be angry because she'd returned to posing in the nude was a farce. Jim knew as well as she did that no woman could be seduced when she was as much in love with her husband as she was with Jim.

Sonia made a grimace of distaste. Certainly not with anyone like Abdul Ahmed.

Not by the widest stretch of her imagination could she conjure up any fantasy lover to whom she might be so attracted that she couldn't control her reactions. And while it was true that she didn't intend ever to be poor again, she simply could not visualize herself going to bed with any man for money. In Acapulco she'd met any number of wealthy men who desired her. Some had told her to name her own fee. One old goat had even offered her a yacht.

How faithful could a wife be?

Sonia turned back to the window. The group in front of the clubhouse was breaking up. She watched Marcia Wilder get into her car. She dried her eyes with the hem of her peignoir and put a fresh pot of coffee on the stove.

Some women drank. Some gambled. Some took lovers. Marcia Wilder was a compulsive gossip. If something had happened in the clubhouse last night that would damage the reputation of one of the residents of the enclave, Marcia would undoubtedly drop in to tell her all of the details.

Chapter Three

As a youth, when he'd earned his living by risking his life four to six times a day diving from La Quebrada, then standing outside the El Mirador in his wet swim trunks to collect the money and gifts admiring tourists forced on him, the matter would have amused Córdoba. So a cute little sixteen-year-old China split tail had waggled her hot little behind in the face of a man or a boy one too many times and had gotten herself raped or stayed with. It happened every night of the year to *muchachas* of every nationality. How old did a girl have to be?

Córdoba wiped his plump jowls with a clean bar towel. He could tell Señor Harris and General Ti things that would pop their eyes, things he'd seen right here at Rancho Paraíso, around the pool, in the cabins of the moored boats and on the beach.

The girl being missing, however, made this different. With the financing of Rancho Paraíso as precarious as it was, twelve of the houses still unsold and another twenty units on the drawing board, he, along with the other developers, couldn't afford any scandal that might affect its sales potential.

Señor Córdoba continued to sweat. According to Mexican federal law no non-national could own or buy any land within fifty kilometers of the coast. That was why when the money men in Acapulco, none of them nationals, had first conceived the enclave, in exchange for the bar and dining-room concession and a small percentage of the eventual net, he'd allowed them to purchase the property in his name. If that fact ever became public knowledge he could well wind up in a federal prison with some other concessionaires getting rich on the spade work he'd done.

Córdoba perspired more heavily at the thought. It was true he had just a small piece of the action but he had a good thing here and he wanted to keep it. He refolded the towel and mopped at his face with the reverse side and tried again.

"Con su permiso, General," he addressed General Ti. "I think this could be too serious a matter for us to decide. I think we should call the *policia* and inform them of the situation."

"I think Córdoba's right," Harris said.

"No," General Ti said. "I don't want the police to be informed. Not for the time being." It was difficult for him to speak so frankly. "If my daughter has been having, shall we say, an indiscretion with one of the youths or men in the enclave, and if she wishes us to believe that something has happened to her in order to delay me from searching for her and bringing her home, Mrs. Ti and I prefer to keep the matter in the family." He paused briefly. "And if she has been harmed I am quite capable of meting out justice."

Harris believed him. Most of the Chinese he'd known were Cantonese, small of stature. But General Ti's ancestry must be Mongol or Manchu. Harris himself stood six feet two and weighed two hundred pounds but Ti was two inches taller and easily outweighed him, all of it solid muscle. Besides, if the rumors he'd heard about Ti were true, the man would have no compunction about slitting the throat of anyone who attempted to harm a female member of his family.

Sitting in one of the wicker chairs in the lounge, deliberately refraining from looking at the stained cushion of the couch beside which her daughter's outer and more intimate garments had been found, Mrs. Ti spoke to her husband in Chinese.

"As you say, my dear," he said gravely, then turned to Harris and Córdoba. "Mrs. Ti suggests that we review the ground we have already covered in the hope of perceiving something we failed to observe the first time. May we begin with you, Señor Córdoba?"

"Si," the portly concessionaire said. "I assure you I have nothing to hide, General. Outside of selling Sally soft drinks at the bar, giving her change for the jukebox, and taking her order when you and Mrs. Ti have favored the dining room with your, I doubt that I've spoken fifty words to Sally. And I spent last night with my family."

"I'm certain you did," General Ti assured him. "But tell us again. What time did you arrive this morning?"

"Shortly after six o'clock."

"Did any of your employees arrive before you did?"

"Si." Córdoba pointed through the glass of the locked door to where Pedro was emptying the accumulated candy-bar wrappers, soft-drink cans and beer cans with the cigar and cigarette butts from the trashcans and sand buckets spaced around the area in front of the clubhouse while Juan skimmed the surface of the pool with a wire net attached to a long, collapsible pole. "Both Pedro and Juan were waiting to help me unload the supplies. They report for duty at six o'clock. Then their wives come in at nine to begin the noon and evening meals and wait on tables."

General Ti said coldly, "I am not interested in their wives. Does either men have a key to the clubhouse?"

"No. I have the only keys. And I am very careful to make certain everything is locked before I leave on the nights I must be away."

"All the doors were locked this morning when you

arrived?"

"*Si.*"

"And it wasn't until after you had supervised the unloading of your supplies that you came in here and discovered my daughter's garments lying beside the couch?"

"*Si.*"

"How did you know they belonged to Sally?"

Córdoba used the folded bar towel again. "I didn't." He indicated the garments. "I merely gathered them up and took them out and showed them to Pepe and Juan and asked them if they knew anything about them. They said they didn't. We were still discussing the affair when Señor Harris arrived. He said they looked like garments he'd seen Señorita Ti wear and suggested we contact you to make sure all was well with her."

Ti turned his attention to Harris. "May I ask how you knew the capri pants and the halter and the panties belonged to my daughter?"

"Oh, come off it, Ti," Harris said hotly. "I know how you must feel, but I told you the first time we went through this that I just remembered seeing Sally wearing a similar outfit. What the hell. I'm either down here or the kids are in and out of my studio half a dozen times a day. Now will you tell me something that hasn't come out so far?"

"If I can."

"If the garments do belong to Sally and Mrs. Ti has identified them, how did they or Sally get down here without you knowing about it?"

"I don't know," General Ti admitted. "As I told you gentlemen, several days ago Sally requested and received our permission to spend a few days in Acapulco as the house guest of a girl friend. She returned home about nine o'clock last night, seeming quite fatigued. Mrs. Ti and I thought she was still in her own room sleeping when Señor Córdoba's employee rang our bell and we discovered she was gone."

"Had her bed been slept in?"

"Yes."

"Well," Harris said, "I suppose it's up to you but I agree with Señor Córdoba. I think we should call the police. Because, with all due respect to Mrs. Ti, judging from the stains on the cushions of the couch and the fact that the garments Córdoba found were probably all Sally was wearing, it seems logical to me that someone enticed her down here and was sexually intimate with her one or more times, with or without her consent."

"And then ...?" General Ti asked.

"I haven't any idea," Harris said. "Maybe she ran away with the guy. Maybe he made sure she wouldn't ever tell anyone what had happened."

General Ti unlocked and opened the door of the lounge.

"Tasy, would you mind stepping in here for a moment?" The red-haired girl came into the lounge wearing a skimpy bikini and drinking a bottle of Coca Cola.

"Yes?" she said.

Ti closed the door and leaned against it. "You're our Sally's best friend, aren't you, Tasy?"

"I guess you could say that," Tasy said. "Why?"

"Then perhaps you can tell us if Sally has any special boy friend in the enclave."

"No," Tasy said. "No boy in particular. You see, mostly we double- or triple-date without paying much attention to who we're with. Then all we do is run the road to Acapulco and maybe go to the movies or drop into Papa Juarez's for a bowl of *pozole* and a coconut milk shake." The girl used her free hand to rub at the bridge of freckles across her nose. "Sometimes with gin. Sometimes without. Depending on how the boys are holding."

"Then you don't know if Sally was having an affair with some boy or man around here?"

"No." The small, plain oval face flashed a grin. "And I wouldn't tell you if I did. Like you say, Sally's my friend."

"How about you, Mr. Harris?" General Ti said.

"What about me?" Harris asked.

"Sally studied art with you two afternoons a week. We know she liked and respected you. Both as an artist and as a man. She's told her mother and me as much on several occasions."

"Make your point."

"Simply this," General Ti said. "Younger girls often confide in older men whom they trust and respect. Did she ever confide in you that she was particularly interested in some special boy in your art classes?"

"Hah," Tasy said. "That's funny. That's really funny, General. There aren't any boys in Mr. Harris' classes. The boys think studying art is sissy." She looked at Harris and added thoughtfully, "But Sally is crazy about Mr. Harris. She thinks he's out of this world." She smiled at Harris. "But then most of the girls do, including me."

"Thanks a lot, Tasy," Harris said dryly. He inclined his head to General and Mrs. Ti. "Now, if you will excuse me, I'll be getting back up the hill. After all, this is not my problem. But I still think you ought to call the police."

He started toward the door of the lounge and

stopped as Juan came in carrying a small object. *"Por favor, Señores,"* the attendant said. "I think this is something you should see. It could have something to do with the missing *Señorita*. It was not in the pool when I cleaned it yesterday morning."

He laid the object on one of the tables. Harris glanced quickly at General Ti and Córdoba. They might not know what kind of a knife it was. He did. It was a palette knife, a blunt-ended semiflexible blade fitted into a wooden handle. It was the type of knife artists use to mix their oils and clean their palettes. What made this one unique was that one side of the blade had snapped off and the remaining steel had been ground down to form a narrow, stiletto-like sliver of metal.

"Ugh," Tasy said. "Maybe something *has* happened to Sally." The bridge of freckles across her nose stood out against her sudden pallor. "Maybe someone used that to make her do it with him, and then did something to her to keep her from telling on him. Gee. Imagine someone pushing something like that into you."

Then, realizing how the statement could be construed, she blushed.

Nothing had changed in the hour that Harris had been gone. The birds, singing lustily now, were fluttering in the branches of the jacaranda tree. Sonia's late-model Toyota roadster and his older-model Plymouth were still in the carport. Whenever he looked over his shoulder the overall scene was just as picturesque as it had been when he'd walked down to the clubhouse to see what was exciting Señor Córdoba. The only thing new was this sudden feeling of breathlessness and possible involvement in what could be a very nasty business.

Since he'd last seen her, Sonia had combed her hair and put on the white peignoir that revealed as much of her lush body as it concealed.

As he entered the kitchen she said, "If you're ready for another cup, there's fresh coffee on the stove. Was there any mail?"

"I forgot to ask," Harris said. He poured himself a cup of coffee and sat across from her and waited for her to question him. When she didn't, he asked, "Well, aren't you curious about what happened down at the clubhouse?"

"I already know," Sonia said. "Marcia stopped in on her way home. Have they called the police?"

"Not yet."

He expected her to pursue the subject. She didn't. Instead, viewing his bare torso through the smoke curling up from the cigarette between her lips, she said, "You might at least have put on a shirt before you went to the clubhouse."

"What's wrong with not wearing a shirt?"

"It doesn't look right."

"Oh, for Christ's sake, Sonia, be reasonable. I wish you'd get over some of those Old World notions of propriety."

Sonia snuffed her cigarette. "I can't help the way I feel.... Well, I suppose it's time for me to dress."

"You're going into town today?"

"I have to. I have a two-o'clock sitting."

"With whom? That phony Abdul Ahmed again?"

"As it so happens, no." Sonia realized the front of her negligée had fallen open and closed it. "But phony or not, Abdul does sell. He's getting as much as five thousand for a canvas."

"He's not selling art," Harris said. "He's peddling

flesh." He attempted to clarify his own position. "Look, honey. I don't want to start another fight. But look at it from my point of view. You object when I walk down to the clubhouse without a shirt. You say, 'It doesn't look right.' How do you think I feel when I pick up one of those magazines you pose for, or walk into someone's rumpus room and there you are, bare bottom, belly and bosoms hanging on the wall."

"You don't have to be so crude about it. Besides, that's different."

"How?"

"I'm a model. And one of us has to earn some money until things start breaking for you again." Sonia's pent-up indignation spilled over. "Now, for all I know, all the time I've been fending off passes, you've been corrupting with a Chinese teenager. And—"

"Don't say that!" Harris said hotly. "Don't even think it. Sally was merely one of my pupils."

"You haven't been having an affair with her?"

"No."

"You still love me?"

"Very much."

"Then why have you been neglecting me for the past two months? Why did you go down to the clubhouse at two o'clock this morning?"

"I don't know."

"You don't remember leaving the house?"

"No."

"But you do remember refusing to have anything to do with me when you returned?"

"Vaguely."

"Why?" Sonia demanded indignantly. "Because you couldn't? Because you'd just stayed with Sally?"

"God no!" Harris said.

"Hah!" Sonia scoffed, and left the room.

Harris sat very still for a while. He refused to consider Sonia's accusation. He might be pushing the barrier but he wasn't that far out of his mind. Drunk or sober, no sane man could be intimate with a girl, with or without her consent, and not remember anything about it.

He walked into the living room in search of cigarettes and paced the huge room trailing a plume of smoke.

Sally Ti was very attractive and well developed for her age. With the exception of Tasy Lane, the Eurasian girl had the most beautiful body of any of the teenagers living at Rancho Paraíso. Possibly because the girl was a combination of the best of two cultures. He would be lying if he denied that he had admired Sally's fresh young beauty in his studio, or lounging around the pool in a bikini. Yes, she had stirred him sexually.

He continued to pace the floor. Unlike a number of men he knew, he'd never been a particular devotee of the nymphet pudenda. The few Lolitas in his life had vanished with his early youth. He'd always preferred mature women. Still, any middle-aged man who claimed that looking at some dewy-eyed teenage girl had never excited him was either an idiot, a liar, or ... Anyway, he could remember at least half a dozen times when Sonia had been the grateful recipient of a flare of passion that one or another of his youthful students had ignited in an art class.

Harris stopped pacing and wiped the perspiration from his face and torso. That would be the final indignity, by God. To be accused of having seduced or raped Sally Ti. And then have to stand in an open court of law and say:

"No. I'm not the man you want. You see, I couldn't have harmed the child. I'm impotent. If you don't believe me, ask my wife."

Harris wiped his palms on his slacks. Maybe he ought to level with Sonia. As painful and embarrassing as the scene would be, maybe he should tell her the real reason for his neglect of his marital obligations.

He would do just that, Harris decided. He'd talk to Sonia after he'd talked to Dr. Gonzales again. The hell of it was, if a man was organically sound—and Gonzales claimed he was—the only real proof of potency or impotency was ability or failure.

Dr. Gonzales claimed it was all in his mind. However, if the condition should prove to be permanent, there was only one thing he could do—give Sonia her freedom. No woman, especially one as young and vital as Sonia, could be expected to live forever with an enfeebled male who approached each new attempt with trepidation, and then either failed her completely, or worse still, aroused her and left her frustrated.

There was, Harris thought, a grim alternative to divorce. If something *had* happened to Sally, and if General Ti decided that he was the responsible male, he wouldn't need a lawyer. The erstwhile General of the People's Army of China would cut his throat.

He glanced at his watch, then walked into the bathroom to shave. Sonia was still in the shower. For some reason, known only to herself, in spite of the fact one of the selling features of the house was an over-sized, sunken, black mosaic-tiled tub, Sonia never used it. She hadn't used it once since they had moved into the house.

As she frequently did, because of the growing morning heat, Sonia hadn't bothered to close the sliding glass door of the shower. Harris studied his wife's reflection in the double mirror over the wash basin as he applied shaving lather to his face.

He'd painted dozens of nudes, either as individual studies or as figures in the larger-than-life murals he'd been commissioned to do by various historical societies and culturally minded municipalities who had wanted their new courthouse or city hall to reflect more than politics. But he'd never painted a more exquisitely formed woman than the blonde Austrian girl who had knocked on the door of his studio one afternoon and announced in her quaint accent that the so and so agency had sent her in response to his telephoned request for a model.

"I'm Sonia von Erlac," she'd told him. "And I don't do anything but pose."

And then, apparently as drawn to him as he had been to her, she had promptly disproved the statement by allowing him to make love to her during their second rest period. And once they had made love the first time, it had been as if the flood gates of a dam had opened for both of them. He'd never subscribed to romantic myths, and yet, actually it was as if neither of them had ever known another man or woman, as if up until the time they'd met they had been waiting for each other.

Harris scraped grimly at the lather on his face. He'd never known one woman could be capable of so much tenderness and passion. If that phase of his life was over, he didn't care what happened to him. He might as well be dead.

He continued to study his wife's reflection in the mirror. Another tribute: he had never known a more fastidious woman. When Sonia finished soaping her body she rinsed and soaped it again, almost as if to cleanse it of some invisible taint. Finally she turned off the water, stepped out on the mat and toweled vigorously.

"How come you're shaving?" she asked him. "Are you going into town?"

"Later," Harris said.

Sonia powdered her body as scrupulously as she'd washed it. She started into the bedroom to dress, then changed her mind and sat on the closed lid of the facility beside the wash bowl.

"May I ask you a question, Jim?"

"Of course."

"Except for that one unpleasant remark I made about Sally Ti—and I don't blame you for being angry with me about that—have I said or done anything to offend you?"

"No."

"Has anyone told you anything about me that has caused you not to—to respect me any more?"

"No."

"And you still love me?"

"Very much."

Sonia folded her hands primly in her lap. "Then why don't you take me into the other room and prove it? I'll call Elsie and tell her to cancel my sitting for this afternoon. I'll tell her I'm not accepting any assignment for two weeks. And we'll spend the entire time trying to work out whatever this is that has come between us. I've tried to be a good wife to you, Jim. I want to keep on being one. But we can't go on this way much longer. Can't you understand? I need you."

Harris' hand trembled so badly he almost cut himself. He was tempted to try. But he was even more afraid of failing, failing as he had on a dozen other days and nights during the miasmic nightmare of the past few months.

"I swear you have no reason to be jealous, Jim.

Please let's stop this nonsense. If you love me, prove it. For both our sakes. Please."

She reached out with one of her fine-boned delicate hands and touched him intimately.

"Please, Jim. Take me in the other room. Let me prove how much I love you."

In physical and mental torment, barely able to keep from being juvenile and spending prematurely, Harris took refuge in masculine indignation. "Now you're talking and acting like a whore," he said hoarsely. "I'll tell you what. When I want to get laid or have any other erotic services performed, suppose I let you know."

Sonia dropped her hand back in her lap, then got to her feet and walked into the bedroom trailing her peignoir behind her. As always when she was angry, her accent grew richer.

"You do that," she purred in a voice like thick velvet. "If there are not too many more important customers in line, I shall see if I can fit you into my schedule."

Chapter Four

The three rooms that comprised the suite of offices were small, on the second floor of an older business block in the maze of narrow streets behind the public market. The gold-leaf letters on the glass door of the reception room read:

HONG KONG IMPORTING AND EXPORTING CO.
SPECIALIZING IN ORIENTAL OBJETS D'ART

Whistling tunelessly as he performed the familiar tasks, General Ti changed the water in the trough of the caged lovebirds and gave them fresh seed.

The knowledge that sooner or later something like this might happen was small consolation. It put him on the sharp horns of a nasty dilemma. If this was a childish prank, if Sally was merely asserting her independence to himself and her mother, he didn't want to embarrass her. If she was in trouble and needed his help, he wanted to be of any assistance he could render. If the child had been harmed, then done away with, in an attempt to conceal the assault on her person, whatever the eventual consequences might be, he intended to kill the man who had harmed her.

In any of the three instances, he couldn't appeal to the local police. The party didn't look kindly on defectors married to White Russian women, especially a defector who'd departed the party discipline with two hundred thousand dollars with which he was supposed to have established credits for badly needed foreign supplies. To be sent back to Red China would mean a firing squad. And even a minor police investigation might uncover a number of things that could lead to his being deported as an undesirable alien.

General Ti used his white silk pocket handkerchief to pat delicately at the perspiration on his smooth jowls. As it was, he'd arrived in Mexico with less than a fourth of the money he'd appropriated. Between cumshaw and *mordida* and the squeeze, as prevalent in the English-speaking jurisdictions through which he'd had to pass as in Mexico or the Orient, when he'd finally reached Acapulco and had been granted political asylum he'd barely had enough money left to make the down payment on the house in *Rancho Paraíso* and sustain himself and his family until he'd been able to put phase two of his plan in operation.

When he'd finished caring for the birds, he put his desk in order, then stood with his massive hands clasped behind his back and stared out the open window at the street scene below while he waited for Charlie Lee and Harry Toy to return to him with their reports.

Except for the physical composition of the buildings, the language being spoken and spelled out on the unlighted neon signs over the various oases of pleasure, he could be viewing a street scene in his native land, the China he'd known as a young man.

The two nations had a great deal in common. Beneath their deceptive cultural crusts the Chinese and the Mexicanos were basically earthy, lusty people who liked to sing and laugh and indulge in all the sensual pleasures made possible by the five senses of man.

From what he'd heard from intimates who'd been there, most of his fellow countrymen in Taiwan still carried on a good number of the old traditions. Ambition could be fatal. He'd made a bad mistake when, during the last days of World War II, he'd traded a lieutenant's commission in the Nationalist Chinese Army for a colonelcy in the irregulars who had become the People's Army of China. He'd been in on the ground floor so to speak. With all of the billions of dollars in economic and military aid the United States had poured into Formosa, instead of being a defector with a price on his head, he could have been a very wealthy man.

He left the window and sat behind his desk as his Mexican receptionist announced over the annunciator that Señores Lee and Toy had returned.

"Nothing," Lee reported. "No one I talked to has heard a thing."

"The same here," Harry Toy said.

Lee sat on the sill of the window fanning his face with the brim of his straw hat. "Look. I realize this is way out, boss. But do you think maybe the Chicago crowd heard about the new shipment and snatched Sally in the hope of cutting in on the deal?"

"I doubt that," Ti said.

Harry Toy agreed with him. "So do I. With things as tight as they are north of the border, the syndicate boys are glad to have a steady source of supply. Besides, if they were putting the arm on us, they would have left a note or something. We'd have been contacted by now."

Charlie Lee admired the razor-sharp crease in the yellow sports slacks he was wearing. "Which puts us back where we started. Like I said this morning, the way I see this thing, some young punk or maybe a man at the enclave got to Sally and persuaded her to run away with him. And they staged the bit in the clubhouse lounge to gain a little time."

General Ti considered the possibility and shook his head. "No. That doesn't stand up. None of the boys or men at the enclave are missing. I made certain of that before I came into town. Were you able to reach the young lady at the address I gave you?"

"Yes, I was," Lee said. He took a small leather notebook from his pocket and read from one of its pages. "Señorita Conchita de Bravo, Bungalows Punta Penasco, Avenida de los Penascos, telephone number 2-20-22."

"I know the young woman's name and address," Ti said curtly. "I gave them to you. What I want to know is what she is like and what she knows about my daughter's current whereabouts."

Lee returned the notebook to his pocket. "She claims

she doesn't know anything about your daughter, that she has met Sally only a few times at a café called The Golden Bull. And that if Sally told you she was to be her house guest or phoned you and Mrs. Ti claiming she was calling from her apartment, she was being untruthful."

"Do you believe her?"

Lee shrugged. "It's difficult to tell when a woman is lying. Especially one as pretty and shapely as Señorita de Bravo. But I did establish the fact that she is a Cuban national, a registered nurse, spending her holidays in Acapulco and, on the surface, there doesn't seem to be any reason why she should have lied to me."

"I'll want to talk to her," Ti said.

"That might be a good idea," Lee said. "But if Sally wasn't with her during the two days she claimed to be, where was she?"

The general took a bottle of Scotch from the bottom drawer of his desk and poured himself a stiff drink in lieu of the breakfast he'd been unable to eat. "I don't have any idea but I intend to find out. And as long as you boys haven't come up with anything in town, it seems to me the best place to begin is back at the Rancho Paraíso. We'll question her young friends and possibly the artist who identified the garments that were found." He drank the drink he'd poured. "Now how about the knife?"

"We did better there," Harry Toy said. He took the handkerchief-wrapped knife from one of his side coat pockets and unwrapped it carefully before laying it on the desk. "It's what is called a palette knife. That is, it was. It is used mostly by artists."

"How do you know?"

Toy shrugged. "That's what the dealer I talked to

said. He told me that artists use them to mix their colors and scrape old paint off their palettes." Toy outlined the original proportions with one finger. "But it should be about a third wider and blunt-ended."

General Ti rewrapped the knife and put it in one of the pockets of his white linen suit. "In that case, I will definitely want to talk to Mr. Harris again." He explained the opening steps of what could be the most important campaign in his life. "I also want to eliminate the possibility that if violence was involved, the perpetrator didn't choose the quickest and most convenient way of concealing whatever took place in the club lounge."

Charlie Lee got up from the window sill. "I don't get you, boss."

"I do," Harry Toy said quietly. "There's a shop just down the street that handles that kind of equipment. And if the kid is in the lagoon or the marina, we'll find her." Toy added quickly, "Not that I think Sally is dead. As pretty as she is, if the knife is connected with her disappearance, I think it is more likely it was used to force her to"—He thought better of what he'd been about to say—"well, let's go pick up some wet suits."

As he drove down Mexico 200 toward its junction with the sand road linking the city with Rancho Paraíso and La Barra de Coyuca, the small fishing village a few miles beyond, to keep his mind occupied, General Ti reflected that there were any number of separate and distinct Acapulcos.

There was the world of the wealthy tourists and equally wealthy Mexican nationalists who occupied the many roomed *palazzos* in the hills and the palatial suites in the luxury hotels overlooking the bay.

There was the world of the less wealthy tourists and their counterparts, the hardworking native middle class, the local business and professional men, the small entrepreneurs as represented by Señor Córdoba.

There was the world of the impoverished squatters who existed in La Laja, the so-called parachutists, because they seemed to drop out of the air to claim the unskilled hotel workers' jobs at coolie wages while their women were happy to work as full-time housemaids for from sixteen to twenty-four dollars a month.

There was the world in which he had his office, a world of neon-lighted signs over cheap nightclubs and *cantinas* in which, to the accompaniment of wailing *mariachi* or blaring brass bands, almost completely nude young girls bumped and ground around a small dance floor, barely managing to keep their G-strings out of reach of the eager hands of the men at the floorside table, while the dancers who had preceded them sat in dimly lighted booths openly allowing their male companions to fondle shapely brown breasts as an inducement to buy them dollar drinks of anise-flavored sugar water for which the girls received a plastic chip worth approximately three *pesos*.

There was, although it had been years since he'd had need to patronize such places, a more unsavory world, so Charlie Lee and Harry Toy had told him. A world of sad-eyed young women, wearing only their *camisas,* who sat in shabby parlors breast-feeding their bastard babies until their services were required, at which time they handed their infants to a companion to care for while, for a small fee, they retired to submit to a meaningless male penetration of their bodies in even shabbier bedrooms hung with religious pictures, and usually a crucifix depicting

Christ's agony hanging over the oil-cloth-covered stand holding the tin wash basin used for prophylactic purposes.

"So help me, boss," Charlie Lee had told him, "you wouldn't believe it unless you saw it. The first time I went into a Mexican house I was so shocked I could hardly jump the broad. It reminded me of stories I've read about the early days on the Barbary Coast in San Francisco. That's when they used to bring our girls over by boatloads, and they had to take on all comers on a 'two-bit lookee,' 'four-bit feelee,' 'six-bit doee' basis."

Ti realized he was gripping the steering wheel too hard. He relaxed and flexed his fingers.

Of course, none of this was applicable to his daughter. As far as he and Olga knew, Sally was a virgin, as pure in mind and body as any well-brought-up sixteen-year-old girl with cultural advantages. Sally's future had been a great factor in his decision to defect. He hadn't wanted his daughter to become a faceless drab in a collectivist society which probably was two generations removed from even the Russian level of development.

On the night he'd decided to defect he had told Olga, "All right, I'm sick of the whole kettle of stinking fish. So are you. But what happens to us isn't too important. We must get our daughter out of here before she's old enough to be married to an I.B.M. computer with a tabulator key for a heart. If we don't, we'll wind up with a file case of statistical reports on the party's next great leap forward instead of a houseful of normal grandchildren."

Now this.

When he reached the enclave he left the white Cadillac Eldorado in the clubhouse parking lot.

"You fellows get started on the lagoon," he said. "I think I'll talk to Tasy first. She and a girl named Brunnhilde have been inseparable since we moved here. And it may be the child was too shocked this morning to tell me everything she knows."

"Whatever you say, boss," Charlie Lee said. "But let's keep our fingers crossed. I'm with Harry. I'll give five to two we don't find a damn thing."

A middle-aged housekeeper answered Ti's knock on the Lane door. *Si*. Both the Señora and the Señorita Lane were at home. The Señora Lane and the new *piloto* whom she had engaged had returned early that morning. They were eating their lunch but under the circumstances, she was sure they wouldn't mind being disturbed.

General Ti believed that his wife had called on Miss Lane, as she preferred to be known, several times. Tasy had been in and out of their house, frequently spending the night with Sally. It was the first time, however, that he'd been in the woman's company. Seen close up, especially after she'd removed the dark sunglasses she affected, Cara Lane was more beautiful than she appeared at a distance or in the motion pictures of her he'd seen.

"How nice, General." She greeted him without rising from her chair at the glass-topped table. "I can't begin to tell you how sorry we all are that your Sally seems to be in some difficulty. What can we do for you?"

General Ti acknowledged her graciousness with a stiff military bow. "If I may, Miss Lane, I would like to talk to Tasy again. The thought has occurred to me that, as one of my daughter's best friends, she may have more to tell me."

Since Ti had last seen her, the red-haired, plain

girl had changed into a low-necked Mexican blouse and a mini skirt that, seen through the glass-topped table, revealed about as much of her firm young thighs as the bikini she'd been wearing.

"Gee, General," she said, "I sure would if I could. But I told you everything I know this morning. Have you found any trace of Sally yet?"

"Not yet."

Cara Lane hesitated, then said, "Look, I don't want to get anyone in trouble but there may be something I can tell you. When Tasy came home she told us that you and Mrs. Ti heard a mild disturbance around two o'clock this morning, and you figure that must have been about the time Sally left her room to meet the person who'd talked her into meeting him in the clubhouse lounge."

"That is correct."

Without bothering to introduce him, the former motion-picture star indicated the deeply tanned, muscular male sitting across the table from her. "Well, it was about two-fifteen this morning when Max and I flew back from the film festival in Mazatlán, when we set down, I saw Jim Harris. Somehow he reminded me of a second-string cameraman who'd just been fired for making time with one of the extras some assistant producer had his eyes on. He was banging and kicking on the door of the club, shouting for someone to let him in. He was so drunk he didn't even notice us when Max and I walked by on the far side of the pool."

"You say this was at approximately two-fifteen?"

"Max can verify the time by his log."

Tasy spooned a mouthful of avocado from her plate, then smiled sweetly at her mother. "It's up to you, General Ti. But if I were you I wouldn't believe a word my mother says. Not about Mr. Harris, anyway. You see, right after we moved in, she made a big play for him. She even wanted to commission him to paint her portrait. But he wouldn't have anything to do with her."

"That's not so, Tasy," the actress said. "It was to be a publicity promotion. And the outfit in Mexico City that was going to make the picture went broke before we could agree on a price."

"Hah," Tasy scoffed. "You make a play for every good-looking man you meet. You even pay them if you have to. With my money. And if he won't lay you, you get sore."

"So help me, Tasy," Cara Lane said, "I mean it. I've taken just about all I'm going to take from you."

"I'm merely telling the truth," her daughter said, and calmly explained to General Ti: "You see, sex is a disease with Mother. She has to have a man every day. Sometimes two or three men. Otherwise she gets wacky."

"That settles it," the actress said. "I'm going to cable that school in Switzerland. Right now. This afternoon. And as soon as they have an opening you're going back. And you're going to stay there until you're twenty-one."

"Like hell I am," Tasy said.

General Ti bowed. "Well, thank you. Thank you all very much. You've been very kind." He backed toward the arch leading to the entrance hall and outer door. "But if you should happen to think of anything, Tasy, anything at all you feel may be pertinent, I will appreciate the information."

The teenager continued to glower at her mother. "If I think of anything I'll let you know, but I can tell you this much right now, General Ti. If something has happened to Sally, something bad, in spite of what my mother said a few minutes ago, I know Mr. Harris didn't have anything to do with it. And when you do find Sally, she'll tell you the same thing."

"May I inquire how you know this?" General Ti asked.

Tasy looked from her mother to him. "Because, well, a lot of old goats around here are always trying to see down your blouse or up under your skirts, or hanging around the pool hoping the strings of your bikini will come untied. But Mr. Harris is always a perfect gentleman. Don't ask me why. I don't know. Maybe because he's so much in love with his wife." She added thoughtfully, "Even if they do seem to be fighting most of the time."

General Ti was interested. "Do you happen to know what they quarrel about?"

"I think," Tasy said, "at least from what I've heard, it has something to do with Mrs. Harris posing buck naked for other artists."

The male of the trio at the table spoke for the first time.

"Hah!" he said. "Posing is a new name for it. I went to a drunken brawl on a yacht over in Puerto Marques Bay and you should see the life-sized oil painting of her the guy had hanging in the master cabin. Not like the pictures in *Playboy,* understand, where all you see are their knockers and their fannies. What I mean all of her was looking you right in the face. And believe me, man, one look at that machine would bring Pancho Villa back to life."

"Oh," Cara Lane said coldly. "And just how did it affect you?"

"Careful, Mother," Tasy warned her. "I wouldn't quarrel with Max if I were you. If you do, he may walk out on you and you won't get your afternoon exercise."

"Suppose you shut your filthy little mouth."

As concerned about his daughter as he was, Ti felt the back of his neck turning red as he continued down the hall with the Mexican housekeeper. As she opened the door for him, he asked, "May I ask if this household is always like this?"

"Most of the time," the woman said.

"Then why do you stay?"

The housekeeper shrugged her thin shoulders. "I am a widow, Señor General, and I have seen and heard all of these things many times. Besides, the pay is good."

Ti considered her answer as he fitted his finely woven panama to his head. It was as logical a reason as any.

Chapter Five

Harris remembered the incident distinctly. Soon after he and Sonia had moved into the enclave he'd tried to pry the staples out of a cardboard carton of new dishes with a palette knife and had snapped the blade.

Palette knives were relatively inexpensive. You could buy one in any shop that stocked artists' supplies. But, on impulse, instead of throwing the knife away, he'd taken it down to the equipment shed and used Juan's foot-propelled grindstone to shape it into a blade suitable for many purposes.

He'd used it to trim canvases and cut old ones out of their frames. He'd used it to cut the ends of cigars and scrape paint from under his fingernails. It could even be used, he supposed, to force a teenage girl to submit to rape.

He searched through the clutter of miscellany on the work table in his studio. Then, failing to find the knife, he lifted the cushions from the chairs and moved the stacks of his unsold finished and unfinished canvases away from the wall and looked behind them.

A half hour later he was still looking. He'd found a half-filled bottle of bourbon that he or Sonia had hidden. He'd found an engraved invitation to an exhibit of modern art at the Acapulco Hilton. He'd found two uncashed checks for two completed mail-order portraits totaling two hundred and fifty dollars. He'd found a number of unpaid bills and a partially used tin of condoms that certainly didn't belong to him and must have fallen from the purse or smock pocket of one of the dewy-eyed young things who studied art with him as a pleasant way of killing time. But the twin of the ground-down knife that Juan had recovered from the pool wasn't in the studio. Nor did it seem likely to him that there could be two such knives.

He gave up his search and looked through the screen door of his studio. The two Chinese in wet suits and snorkels had finished fine-combing the bottom of the lagoon. And now, while several residents of the neighborhood looked on, they were beginning to comb the marina, paying particular attention to the areas under the buoys to which the larger boats were moored.

Harris bought himself a small drink from the bottle he'd found. He'd thought his nerves couldn't become any more jangled than they'd been following the scene with Sonia and her sullen departure. He'd been wrong. All it had taken was the sight of General Ti, placidly fanning his face with his hat as he walked up the road from the clubhouse, pausing briefly before the house, and then, in a variation of the old Chinese water torture, continuing up the road to the Wilder home. Only God and the two women knew what Sonia had told Marcia Wilder, and what Marcia in turn had told General Ti.

Harris sat in one of the chairs his students used and tried to recall as much as he could of the preceding night. He remembered getting drunk. He remembered quarreling with Sonia. After Sonia had mentioned the incident in their earlier conversation, he remembered storming out of the house and weaving down the street to the clubhouse, so filled with self-pity he'd been as high on emotion as he'd been on whiskey. He remembered coming back to the house and going to bed when Sonia snuggled into his arms and said she was sorry if she'd said or done anything to offend him, her hands moving busily between them as she tried to excite him. He remembered turning his back on her. But what had happened from the time he left the house until his return was a complete blank. It could be his old trouble had started again.

"Traumatic amnesia," the army psychiatrist had called it.

That had been after a nasty stretch of fighting on the heights overlooking the Imjin River, north of Seoul, when the Reds had thrown everything they had at the Eighth Army's Third Infantry Division and they'd pushed each other back and forth for two days.

He distinctly remembered the four-hour artillery barrage preceding the push. He'd been one of a team manning a light machine gun, the other two men being Red Faver and Bill Meyers, with whom he had fought his way back from the Yalu debacle when Red

China had first entered the war. He could hear again the bugles and whistles signaling the attack. He remembered Faver and Meyers buying the farm, both victims of a grenade thrown by a Red Chinese soldier who had infiltrated the line. He remembered shooting the Red Chinese soldier with Meyers' rifle and then firing in short bursts at what seemed to be hundreds of moving bodies etched against the night sky where the ridgeline and sky joined. And once again he heard the hollow clang that told him he was out of ammo and he'd better bug out while he could.

Harris ran his fingers through his graying hair. But even now, sixteen years later, he still didn't remember that, instead of bugging out as any man in his right mind would have done, he had clamped his bayonet onto his M-l and scrambled out of the foxhole, offering to take on the whole slope-head army in hand-to-hand combat. According to the citation they'd given him he'd done just that.

Whenever he thought of it—and he tried to think of it as infrequently as possible—it still gave him an eerie feeling to know that two days had been torn out of his life as a man might tear two pages from a calendar.

"You're an art student in civilian life, aren't you, soldier?" the psychiatrist at Walter Reed had asked him.

"Yes, sir."

"Then don't feel so badly about a little lapse of memory. To many men fighting and killing is merely an extension of their normal personalities. They are accustomed to using violence to settle their differences in civilian life. But while I see from your record that you've been an excellent soldier, you're basically a gentle and sensitive man. And seeing men you knew and liked being killed and then being forced to kill other men you didn't know was such a shock that your conscious mind rejected it. But now you're back in the mainstream again and I doubt that any permanent damage has been done."

Traumatic amnesia. It was as good an explanation as any. But if it had happened once it could happen again. If it explained his two-day blackout in Korea, it could explain what had happened last night.

During his first consultation with Dr. Gonzales, the specialist had told him he couldn't find anything organically wrong and he believed the trouble was all in Harris's mind. Maybe he was working too hard, worrying too much or possibly drinking too much. All three could be contributing factors to diminishing sexual prowess. But Dr. Gonzales had also told him that nature's best cure for sagging virility was the application of the *glans penis* to the puckered, pink *labia minora* of a young and pretty girl. If that didn't help, Dr. Gonzales said, nothing would.

Harris built a case against himself. Sally was young. She was pretty. What if she'd been having an affair with one of the men or boys in the enclave and had sneaked out of her room and walked down to the clubhouse to meet him? Then, before the meeting could take place, he'd staggered to the bar in search of more whiskey and, drunk as he'd been, fresh from another failure with Sonia and determined to prove himself a man, he'd held the palette knife to the child's throat and attempted to rape her. Then, failing with her as he had with his wife, something inside him snapped. And then, to cover his inadequacy, to protect his image as a man, he'd killed her and disposed of her body.

Gentle and sensitive or not, he was capable of killing. He had a Silver Star to prove it.

Still, that didn't make sense. While there was no way of proving what had taken place on the couch in the lounge, he had no doubt that a chemical analysis of the stains on the cushion and on the pink rosebud-embroidered panties would prove that at least one and possibly two intimacies had taken place.

He looked at his watch and stood up. In his search for the knife he'd moved most of the canvases away from the wall and stacked them helter skelter. Before dressing to drive into Acapulco he started to restack them—and uncovered a small oil painting. Something about it puzzled him.

He stood the picture on his work easel and studied it. He'd painted it sometime toward the end of last month. Late one afternoon, when he'd had no classes or other painting to do, he'd walked down to the bar to add a few drinks to his tab. Passing the pool he'd seen Sally Ti, Tasy Lane and Brunnhilde Schiller sunning themselves on the inflated pads.

The Chinese girl had been lying with her knees drawn up resting a book on them—a slim volume of Elizabeth Barrett Browning's *Sonnets from the Portuguese*. Tasy had been looking pensively up at the sky. Brunnhilde had been sprawled on her back, her plump thighs spread-eagled in youthful abandonment, shielding her eyes from the sun with the back of a plump arm.

Framed as they were against the blue of the bay and the lacy green of a clump of young traveler's palms, the trio had offered a delightful, once-in-a-lifetime composition. The idea had occurred to him immediately. Why not paint the three girls in a modified version of the type of rumpus-room art that so many local artists were selling like *tacos*? He could title the picture *The Three Graces*, and if he did a good job it probably would sell for enough to give him a financial breather.

To that end, without their knowledge, he'd sketched the three girls in pencil, then returned to his studio and started to enlarge the study on canvas in oil.

The completed picture had turned out charming, with only a faint hint of the Faith, Hope and Charity double entendre he had in mind. When he'd shown it to Sonia she'd said it was one of the best things he'd done in years. But she'd also pointed out that all three of the girls were minors and unless he could get permission from their parents to display and offer the picture for sale, he could be leaving himself wide open for an invasion-of-privacy lawsuit that would cost more in legal fees than he could get for the picture.

But this picture on the easel was not the oil he'd painted. It had been retouched into a travesty. Now it was more pornographic than anything that Abdul Ahmed offered for sale. In this canvas, the skimpy bikinis the three girls had been wearing had been painted out and they were completely nude from the peaked nipples of their young breasts down to the most intimate details of their anatomical division. In addition, what he'd meant to be wistful expressions on their faces had been painted into lewd and salacious invitation.

This wasn't the work of an amateur. Who ever had retouched this picture knew his business.

Harris laid the canvas face down on his work table. He wrapped it in a double layer of heavy brown paper and secured the paper with stout cord.

This introduced a new element into his relationship with Sonia. With things already as bad as they were, she wouldn't be pleased to have him intrude on a sitting. But he had to talk to her as soon as possible.

He wanted to know when she'd last seen the ground-down palette knife that had been on his work table. More important, he wanted to know what professional artist had been given access to his studio since he'd painted the original version of *The Three Graces*.

Cara Lane probably wouldn't care. Being as much of a slob as her daughter, Mrs. Schiller would find the picture amusing. But if General Ti stopped in to question him further and found the canvas in his studio ....

Chapter Six

The view as one entered Acapulco proper never failed to impress Harris. He liked its great splotches of color. The background could be a painting by Gauguin, using his colors unmixed just as they'd been pressed out of the tubes. Against that, the broad, palm-tree-lined boulevard curving around the bay in which the Spanish had first anchored their galleons in 1521 and the scores of multi-balconied homes and luxury hotels set into the rocky cliffs overlooking the water, made the sprawling resort city look more like the French Riviera than the working seaport it had once been.

The radiator of his eight-year-old Plymouth was steaming and hissing so he coasted down the rest of the hill in neutral, then drove slowly to the garage just off the Zocalo where he and Sonia had their cars serviced.

"It's your water pump," the mechanic informed him. "You're going to have to have a new one."

"*¿Quánto?*" Harris asked.

"I'd say about twenty-eight bucks, U.S.," the man

said. "And don't give me that *es mucho* bit. I'll be lucky if I can find a pump to fit an antique like this."

It was an expense Harris hadn't counted upon. It was almost three o'clock. He would have to ask either Elsie or Papa Juarez to cash one or both of the checks he'd found.

"Okay. Put one on. I'll be back in about two hours."

As along the Avenida Presidente Aleman and in almost every other section of the city, there were new ultramodern buildings on the streets surrounding the central plaza. But the Zocalo had changed less dramatically than the rest of the town. The shade from the flowering red and purple jacaranda trees still gave it an illusion of coolness. Wandering bands of *mariachis* and urchin street salesmen and old ladies selling *rebozas* still peddled their wares. Sharp-eyed young men still sat sprawled on the benches strumming their guitars, alternating their attention between the legs and swishing skirts of the passing girls and the faces of less self-assured *turistas* who looked as if they might need the services of a guide.

Harris crossed the Zocalo and rode an elevator in the new office building up to Dr. Gonzales' fifth-floor office. The brittle brunette in the stiffly starched uniform of a nurse was desolated to see him. "Oh, I am so sorry, Señor Harris," she greeted him in Spanish. "I was supposed to phone you and cancel your appointment."

"Then Dr. Gonzales isn't in?"

"No. He isn't even in town. He flew up to El Paso late yesterday afternoon to speak at a medical convention and he won't be back until the day after tomorrow." She added hopefully, "Is there anything I can do for you?"

"No. I doubt that," Harris said. "Well, I'll phone for

another appointment."

"Please do. And *gracias*. Thank you for not being angry with me for forgetting to call you."

"De nada," Harris said rather wryly.

He rode down in the elevator and recrossed the square, clasping the brown paper parcel under one arm.

Sonia's agent's office was on the far side of the public market, on the edge of the legalized red-light district. It was in the same block as a tourist strip joint with a twenty-five-peso minimum. There was a bongo factory, a woman's shop catering to locals and a closed travel bureau on the ground floor of the building. A yellowed and weathered three sheet extolling El Mirador Hotel and the cliff divers of La Quebrada had been posted over the grimy window of the closed travel bureau.

As Harris climbed the stairs he mused that, after the financial dive he'd taken for the last two years, the cliff diving at La Quebrada would be old hat. It would be nice to eat at El Mirador again. When he and Sonia had first moved to Acapulco, El Mirador had been one of their favorite drinking and dining spots.

The offices on the second floor of the building were occupied in the main by artists' representatives and small-time theatrical agents who supplied singers and musicians to the cheaper supper rooms and nightclubs. The offices were strung together by a series of small rehearsal rooms that could be rented by the hour.

Elsie Fillmore's office was at the end of a long hall. To reach it, Harris had to pass a number of the rehearsal rooms. Because of the heat most of the doors were open. In one of the rooms a slim Mexican girl, wearing an abbreviated practice costume, was rehearsing a dance routine to the tinkle of an upright piano that needed tuning. In another a blonde girl was sitting cross-legged on a high stool accompanying herself on a guitar as she recorded a native folksong. A message pad hung from a hook beside Elsie Fillmore's door. That meant the agent was not in her office, and the pad lacked any notation as to when she might return.

Harris walked back down the stairs. He crossed the street to a small neighborhood *cantina* from which he could see the entrance to the office building and ordered a bottle of beer.

It was served by a sleepy-eyed girl in a startlingly pink dress. "You buy me a drink?" she asked.

"Not today," Harris said.

The girl itched and scratched where she itched. "Maybe you like to go somewhere with me? I show you ver' good time."

"Not today," Harris repeated.

The girl shrugged, then yawned and returned to the rear booth in which she'd been sleeping.

Harris sipped his beer, pondering the scene back at the enclave when he'd dropped in to buy a package of cigarettes and see if there was any mail before starting out in search of Sonia.

Señor Córdoba had been very cordial. But the same hadn't been true of the surf-board and bikini set. The silence that greeted his entrance had been deafening. Then when Córdoba had remarked he was still of the opinion that General Ti should report Sally's disappearance to the police and he'd agreed with Córdoba, young Carlson had turned on his stool and glowered at him.

"I'll bet. I'll just bet you do."

"Please, Mr. Harris," Tasy, who'd been sitting next

to him, had said quickly, "don't pay any attention to Andy. He's drunk."

The large veins in Harris' temples resumed their throbbing. "You stay out of this," Andy had warned her, then waggled his finger in Harris' face. "Do you want me to tell you what I think happened in there last night?"

"Please do," Harris had told him. And young Carlson had.

"I think you had another fight with your wife last night and she wouldn't give you any. So you staggered down here and found Sally. You thought to yourself, why not? And when the kid wouldn't put out, you held that goddamn knife to her throat and forced her. A kid in her condition. You didn't even care if she was part Chinese. All she was to you was a piece of tail. Then after you got what you wanted, you either did something to her to keep her from telling her father or she was so ashamed she ran away. She's probably hiding somewhere right now, bawling her eyes out."

It was about as ironic a situation, Harris thought, as it could be. What was he supposed to tell the punk? That he couldn't possibly have harmed Sally, that he couldn't even take care of his own homework?

And what had Andy meant by "A kid in her condition"?

Harris mulled over the remark as he ordered another beer.

"Cerveza."

"Si, Señor," the bar man said, then called, "Lupe," and the Mexican girl in the tight pink dress went into her act again.

"You like to buy me a drink, *Señor?*"

"No."

"Maybe you like to go somewhere with me? I show

you ver' good time."

"Just the beer, *por favor*," Harris said.

"What's the matter? You no like girls?"

"Not at the moment," Harris admitted.

Three more beers and two hours later, with the afternoon shadows beginning to lengthen and the neon signs beginning to wink on, Harris wondered if he'd missed seeing Elsie enter the building so he recrossed the street and climbed the stairs again.

His luck was holding. There was, he discovered, a rear entrance to the building. While he'd sat waiting for her, Elsie had picked up her messages and presumably left for the day.

The Golden Bull was one of a number of partly open-air restaurants on the Calle La Paz. The only thing that differentiated it from the others was the large number of artists who patronized it. It was inexpensive and if their GI checks or money orders from home were late, Papa Juarez, as his contribution to culture and the arts, would allow his established customers to run tabs.

He could afford to. He was known to own two hotels, a piece of the local bull ring and a working silver mine.

What entertainment there was was spontaneous: a bearded youth reading a tone poem; a sweet young thing who'd had too many green coconuts doing an impromptu fertility dance on one of the tables while two future Diego Riveras or David Alfaro Siqueiros quarreled over which one of them was going to walk her back to her room and assist her in completing the rites; some earnest young soul trying to explain his conception of existentialism, how he knew God was dead or arguing vehemently that Juan O'Gorman's ten-story-high wrap-around mosaic blanketing the main library of the University in Mexico City was one of the seven wonders of the modern world while his opponent argued just as vehemently that the mural was much too stylized and decadent upper-lower middle-class garbage.

Harris found an unoccupied table in the garden section. On several occasions Sonia had mentioned she'd stopped by for a drink and to say hello to Papa but it had been almost six months since he was at The Golden Bull. That had been on the afternoon he'd driven half a dozen of his giggling students into Acapulco to view an exhibit. Then, because he thought they might enjoy a touch of Bohemia and it didn't cost very much, he'd treated them to dinner and brown coconuts at The Golden Bull.

He leaned the paper-wrapped canvas against one of the legs of the table and ordered a bowl of *pozole*, the thick soup made of corn, black beans, onions and pieces of chicken or pork, partly because it only cost eight *pesos* and partly because, in spite of the beer he'd drunk, he was hungry.

While he was eating, Papa spotted him under the trees and came over and sat at his table. "It's been a long time, Jim, too long," the fat man said as they shook hands. "How are things with you?"

"Not so good," Harris admitted. "But before you go away, Papa, there are two things I'd like to ask you. Do you know Elsie Fillmore's telephone number or address? And will you cash a couple of checks for me?"

Juarez took his wallet from his pocket. "I'll be happy to cash any check with your endorsement on the back. But I haven't any idea where Elsie is living." The fact seemed to amuse him. "I seldom ever see her any more, now that her agency is beginning to pay off. I suppose she's afraid being seen here will jeopardize her standing with the jet set."

"That could be," Harris agreed.

He endorsed the checks and laid them on the table. When Juarez counted his cash, having deposited the previous night's receipts late that afternoon, he found he was four hundred *pesos* short of covering the total but said he would be happy to give Harris the balance if he would drop back in an hour or so.

"I'll be glad to," Harris said. "This will save me another trip into town in the morning. And thanks."

"My pleasure." The fat man leaned across the table and lowered his voice to a confidential whisper. "Look. I suppose this isn't any of my business but you aren't mixed up in this thing, are you, Jim? That isn't the reason Sonia was crying when she was in here last week?"

"Mixed up in what thing?" Harris asked.

"This business concerning that part-Chinese girl you brought in here some months ago. I hear she's run away from home, that there is some suspicion she was raped or was having an affair with some man and that's why she took off."

"Who told you that?"

Papa pointed to a table partially hidden by the trunk of a tree. "Señorita Schiller and the young man with her. They came in about half an hour ago with Cara Lane's daughter. And when I asked them where the Chinese girl was that usually came in with them, they told me about that business out at Rancho Paraíso."

"No," Harris said, "I'm not mixed up in it. All I did was identify the garments that were found as ones I'd seen Sally wearing."

"Good," Papa Juarez said. "And things are all right

between you and Sonia?"

"Fine. Just fine," Harris lied.

He waited until the fat man had moved to another table, then put the money in his wallet. Well, he knew one man who could tell him Elsie's address. He might even know where Sonia was.

He made his way between the tables to where Brunnhilde and Herman Gottlieb were sitting.

"You must like this place. I gather from Papa Juarez that you come here often."

Brunnhilde sipped the gin-laced coconut milk shake in front of her. "That's right. Ever since you first brought us here. Usually once or twice a week. That's why we drove in tonight. We thought if nothing has happened to her, you know, if Sally has just run away or something, we might find her here."

"I understand Tasy drove in with you."

"Yes, sir," young Gottlieb said. "But when we didn't find Sally, she decided to go to a movie."

Harris started to leave and turned back. "By the way, how did you make out with Andy? Did you get him sobered up before his father came home?"

Brunnhilde moved her head from side to side. "No. And was that an icky scene. I almost wish I hadn't made it. You know how Mr. Carlson is." She drew a square in the air with her forefinger. "And when he came home and found Andy drunk and blubbering because he was afraid something had happened to Sally, he took off for wayoutville. He said he couldn't be more pleased if something had happened to her because he was goddamned if he wanted any part-Chinese brat in his family."

"Would you explain that?" Harris asked.

Brunnhilde returned her attention to her gin milk shake.

"Figure it out for yourself, Mr. Harris."

"Sally is pregnant?"

Brunnhilde made a slurping noise with her straw. "I haven't any idea." She added, without malice, "But ever since Andy stopped holding hands with Tasy about three months ago, he and Sally have been awfully close."

"Has anyone told General Ti or Sally's mother what you've just told me?"

"No," Herman said. "We don't know for sure that's why Sally's been so nervous and upset lately. Besides, why should we get Andy into trouble?"

Chapter Seven

This high in the hills early evening was pleasantly cool, perfumed with the scent of flowers and spiced with the salt of the sea.

From where Harris stood on the flagged terrace, waiting for Abdul Ahmed to answer the ornate knocker on the over-sized door studded with brass nails, he could look out and down and see the lights of Acapulco twinkling like diamonds scattered by the hand of a petulant child. And beyond the lights in the wooded hills and rocky cliffs were the harbor lights and those in the private yachts and luxury hotels rimming the beaches.

This was the other Acapulco. The Acapulco of white dinner jackets and evening gowns and nine-thirty ten-course dinners. The world of swank supper clubs and name bands. This was the way he liked to live. This was the way he and Sonia had lived before things had gone sour for him and he'd attempted to retrench by sinking what money he'd had left in the house at

Paraíso Bay, then wound up going deeply into debt to furnish it and to pay for the incidentals he'd been unaware went with becoming a householder.

He banged the knocker again and heard a scuff of slippered feet on the tile on the far side of the door. Ahmed claimed to be Turkish. Harris doubted it. More likely he was a Levantine. He could be Greek or Lebanese or Syrian. He did know the man was a talented artist, had a bad name where women were concerned and habitually wore a red fez with a golden tassel. It was said to conceal the fact that he was prematurely bald.

He was wearing the fez now, a pair of red leather slippers with turned-up toes and a rich-looking red silk dressing gown. The hairy legs between the bottom of the dressing gown and the top of the red slippers were bare.

"I trust I interrupted something," Harris said.

"You did," Ahmed assured him. "But then that usually happens on my housekeeper's night off." He indicated the paper-wrapped canvas under Harris' arm. "Don't tell me you dropped in to have a real artist give you an opinion on a piece of trivia you've painted?"

"No," Harris said. "All I want from you, if you have it, is Elsie Fillmore's home telephone number or address."

"I'm disappointed." Ahmed smiled. "When I saw you standing on the patio, my mind immediately jumped to two conclusions. You wanted my advice. You'd come to beat me up. So many husbands do. Want to, that is." He led the way down a picture-hung hallway. "Okay. Come into the workshop. I don't recall the broad's number offhand but it should be in my address book."

Ahmed's studio was about what Harris expected.

The room was huge, made of white adobe brick and timber, with a cathedral ceiling. The entire north wall was glass, with a one-hundred-and-eighty-degree view of the bay and the city. Soft music, presumably issuing from a hi-fi, was welling from behind a partially closed door at the far end of the studio.

As his fellow artist sorted through the disorder of pencil sketches, half-used tubes of paint and other clutter on his desk, Harris studied the life-size oil on the easel. It was obviously the latest in Ahmed's series of what was becoming classic back-bar and rumpus-room nudes.

There was no denying the man's talent. His knowledge of anatomy was sound. There was a Renoir quality to his flesh tints. The pictured girl, sullen-eyed, smoke curling from a cigarette dangling from one corner of her moist and parted lips and standing with her feet apart and her lower body thrust forward and completely nude except for a pair of diaphanous pastel-green harem pants that accentuated the sparse copper-colored hair on her detailed *mons veneris,* looked as if she were about to step out of the canvas and into the beholder's waiting arms and bed.

Ahmed paused in his search for his address book. "What do you think of it, Harris?"

"It's good," Harris admitted. "It's one of the best-executed nudes I've ever seen. Also one of the filthiest. Anyone who would hang a picture like that in any room of his house would sell his own mother."

"Oh, come off it, Harris. Stop playing John the Baptist and crawl into bed with Salome. As the saying goes, it only hurts a little while. Recognize the trend. In art. In literature. On the stage. In motion pictures. In everyday life. God and bourgeois morality died two weeks ago last Tuesday and the whole world has gone on a sex binge. The Great God Cock has become the Golden Calf, the parted vulva the gateway to Olympus. And *Mene, Mene, Tekel, Upharsin* doesn't mean 'Thou are weighed in the balance and found wanting.' The new translation is 'Get yours while the getting is good.'"

"Aren't you mixing your metaphors?"

"That may be. But that doesn't make my point any less valid. The fact remains that while you have a lot better reputation in art circles than I have, you're sweating out a living teaching art and painting mail-order portraits, while I'm traveling with the carriage trade." He paused in his search for the book to glance at the door from which the music was coming. "Then, of course, there's the lagniappe."

Harris continued to study the life-sized nude. It could be his trouble was mental; viewing the girl's body both excited and disgusted him. But one thing about the painting seemed artistically wrong. The girl's face, especially her eyes, was too old for her lush body. It appeared as if Ahmed had used two models.

Ahmed found his address book. "Here it is." He wrote Elsie Fillmore's home address and phone number on a card and gave it to Harris. "I don't suppose it's any of my business why you want to get in touch with Elsie after office hours?"

"No," Harris said.

Ahmed took a box of cigarettes from the pocket of his dressing gown and lighted one without offering the box to Harris. "Don't tell me Sonia has finally walked out on you and you're trying to locate her through Elsie?"

Harris refused to be baited. "I don't see that our personal life is any of your business."

"No," Ahmed admitted. He seemed to be trying to

come to a decision. He made it. "Look, Harris. I have no particular reason to like or dislike you. But I do happen to like your wife. I also know from remarks she's dropped that you aren't very happy about her returning to modeling. So, in case you two are going around, because I do like her, I'm going to tell you something."

"I'm listening."

Ahmed reached into the pocket of his robe again, took out a small pearl-handled revolver, displayed it briefly and returned it to his pocket. "Just in case," he smiled thinly, "I should say something you don't like. I have a built-in complex about being mauled by jealous husbands or boy friends."

"Go on," Harris said coldly. "You've either said too much or too little."

Ahmed filled his lungs with the acrid smoke of the cigarette he'd inserted into a carved ivory holder. "As you know, Sonia has modeled for me a dozen times these last few months. And every time she's posed, what do you think she's talked about? You.

"I've spent some time in Vienna. I know she comes from there. I've tried to get her to talk about her early days. How things were during the four-power occupation. How beautiful the Ringstrasse is in the spring with all the trees beginning to leaf out. The *Studentkellers* where the local cats and artists hang out. But will she talk about Vienna? No. Her life begins with you. All she ever talks about is what a wonderful husband and lover you are and how happy she is out at Rancho Paraíso and how, even if you have struck a dry spell, you are the greatest thing that's ever happened to the art world since Jim Whistler bought his mother a rocking chair."

"That sounds like a rather one-sided conversation."

"It always is," Ahmed said rather grimly. "Except for the one time, the second time she posed for me. I didn't know her very well then. After we finished for the day Sonia went into the dressing room to put on her street clothes. I followed her in."

Ahmed's cigarette had gone out. He relit it. "And there she was, sitting on the edge of the bed, just finished with putting on her stockings, snugging a wide red garter with a big red bow in place. When she looked up and saw me, what did she do? She 'eeked' like a goosed virgin, by God. Held one arm over her breasts and clapped her other hand over that honey-colored pussy of hers."

Ahmed sighed.

"Naturally, I thought she was putting on an act, so I sat down beside her to warm her up a little. But before I could get going she jumped to her feet and snatched up her purse and took out the goddamnedest knife I'd ever seen. Then, standing there stark naked except for her stockings and those damn red garters, she assured me it was nothing personal. She said she admired me as an artist and imagined I would be an excellent lover. But she also said that she'd never been unfaithful to you, and never intended to be, and if I didn't keep what was bothering me properly in my pants behind a properly zipped fly, she intended to do her best to cut it off."

"And then?"

"I believed her," Ahmed said. "Oh, I did take the knife away from her. But only to salve my pride. Then I got the hell out of there and let her dress."

"You give up easily, don't you?"

"Usually no. Normally I'd have made an issue of it. But in that instance it was a matter of economics. I didn't want Sonia to get so sore she'd refuse to pose for me. What the hell, Harris. You know the local situation. A piece of tail per se is cheaper than green coconuts. And about as hard to get. From the pro stuff down in the district to the stupid little broads who hang around places like The Golden Bull, to the vacationing secretaries from Brooklyn or Des Moines who reason what they do in Acapulco doesn't count. I can get all of that I want for the asking. But I got five grand, forty thousand lovely *pesos* for the last canvas I did of Sonia."

Harris nodded slowly. "I don't suppose you remember what type of a knife Sonia used to defend herself?"

"Very distinctly. It looked like a palette knife. One of yours, possibly. One you'd broken and ground down to cut or trim canvas."

"Do you know where it is now?"

"I haven't any idea. I remember tossing it on the hi-fi in the dressing room but I haven't seen it or thought of it since. Sonia probably put it back in her purse after I left the room."

Harris studied the Turk's face. It seemed to be without guile. There was no reason that Ahmed should tell him what he had unless he meant to be helpful. On impulse, he unwrapped the altered canvas.

"While I'm here, I'd like you to look at this."

Ahmed whistled his appreciation as he studied the painting of the three girls. "Say. This is good. Who did it?"

"I did. At least I painted the original."

"Welcome to the club."

"But this isn't the way I painted it, Ahmed. All three girls were wearing bikinis in the original. Excluding what you know of my work, do you happen to recognize the brush work in the alterations?"

Ahmed turned on a work light and held the canvas under it. "No, I can't say I do. Those flesh tints could be mine." He shrugged. "Or, for that matter old Max Arnold's or Dimitri's." He gave the painting back to Harris. "We both know almost any professional artist can copy another artist's style. But why would anyone want to alter a painting of yours—and how did the party get hold of it?"

Harris rewrapped the oil and secured the paper with the cord. "That's what I'm trying to find out. Well, thanks for Elsie's address."

Ahmed's voice was slightly mocking. "Think nothing of it. I'm always happy to be helpful to a fellow craftsman." He glanced at the partially closed door at the end of the studio. "Now, if you have everything you want, I'll get back to what I was doing when you banged on my front door. Do you want me to show you out?"

"No, thanks. I can find my way," Harris said.

When he reached his car, he shifted the canvas to his other arm preparatory to opening the door, then looked over his shoulder as two well-dressed, muscular-looking Chinese stepped out from behind a huge bougainvillea bush growing beside the road.

"Am I addressing Mr. James Harris?" one of the men asked politely.

"That's right," Harris said. "I'm Jim Harris."

"Fine." The Chinese smiled. "As they say in this country, *por favor*. General Ti would like to talk to you."

"About what?"

"His daughter, Sally Ti."

Harris shook his head. "I'm sorry. I don't know a thing more about it now than I did when I talked to him this morning."

Harry Toy reached past him and opened the door of the Plymouth. "Let's let the general be the judge of that. Get in and drive, Mr. Harris. I'll ride with you and Charlie can follow in our car."

BOOK TWO

With nightfall, while Acapulco proper comes even more alive, while romance, stimulated with exotic tropical drinks, dances under the stars to throbbing Latin melodies and the strumming of a thousand guitars, the tourist activities on Los Hornos Beach cease and the native fishermen take over, each man fishing his traditional portion of the bay. It is estimated that five hundred native fishermen reap a nightly harvest of five tons of fish, of which Acapulco consumes three tons while the rest is shipped to Mexico City in refrigerated trucks over the new superhighway that has replaced the narrow burro trail winding through the mountains that was once the only link between the cities.

Chapter Eight

The decrepit-looking black ketch tugging gently at its mooring ropes was sixty feet long, diesel-powered, deceptively fast for its appearance. The night wind off the ocean had been blowing for an hour but with all the portholes except the one on lee side closed, it was dark and stiflingly warm in the forward cabin when the black-haired girl on the built-in bunk awakened.

Her pulse was pounding. She felt as if thousands of curious ants were crawling all over her body. She tried to brush them away and couldn't.

She fought down a desire to scream. She swung her bare feet to the floor and crossed the unlighted cabin to the open porthole and looked out. The ketch was still moored in the bay. In the distance she could see the double stream of headlights of the cars on Costera Miguel Aleman, and, closer, the dim yellow lanterns and running lights of the small boats of the local fishermen as they fished their portions of the bay.

It had been early evening the last time she'd looked. Now it was night and Charlie Lee still hadn't come to take her to the doctor he knew. After he'd promised. After she'd done what she had to prove she was grateful for what he was trying to do for her.

Even though it was almost eighteen hours distant and she'd had all day to think, the early-morning scene on the couch in the lounge of the clubhouse at Rancho Paraíso was as confused in her mind as the events of the night on which the whole business had started.

After she'd sneaked out of the house to meet him and he'd given her an injection of the medicine on which she was becoming more and more dependent, Charlie Lee had told her, "You know as well as I do what will happen if your father finds out that I've been trying to help you. He'll kill me. He'll blow off my head with that forty-five he always carries. So how about trying to prove your gratitude and giving me a break? After all, in your condition, what difference does it make?"

Sally pressed one of her flushed cheeks to the cool metal rimming the porthole. Her face tightened as she continued her thoughts. Because she'd been so desperate, because all three of the doctors in Cuernavaca to whom Conchita had sent her had refused to do what she had to have done and because Charlie Lee had sworn he knew a doctor right here in Acapulco who would, she'd let him do what he wanted to do, had wanted to do ever since he and Conchita had first started giving her the daily injections he and the Cuban nurse had sworn were certain to terminate her pregnancy and force her to have a miscarriage.

After she'd let him undress and handle her, hating every minute of it, wishing she was dead, she'd let him be intimate with her twice before they'd left the club, the second time with Mr. Harris pounding on the locked door of the bar and demanding that Señor Córdoba open up and sell him a bottle of bourbon. Then once again, after he'd brought her here. And that time he hadn't even asked her permission. He'd just stripped off the capris and halter he'd bought her to replace those she'd left beside the couch in the lounge and had pushed her back on the bunk as if she were a ten-peso whore.

"It will relax you, honey," he'd told her. Now it was night again and he hadn't come back to take her to the doctor.

She pushed herself away from the open porthole and felt her way through the dark to the metal wash basin and filled it with tepid water. Then, after squirming out of her pants and halter she tried, without success, to wash away the invisible ants.

Even with her body slick with water, her skin felt dry and lifeless. The ants continued to crawl, and equally as bad, if not worse, the cramps and nausea were beginning again. Without bothering to put on the garments she'd discarded, she sat back on the bunk doubled over with pain. She'd read and heard other girls say that having a baby could be very unpleasant and some girls had more trouble than others. But she hadn't expected to feel so bad so soon. After all, she was only three months pregnant.

Hugging herself with both arms to keep from

scratching at the itch that tormented her, she rocked back and forth on the bunk. Why had this happened to her? She didn't even particularly like Andy Carlson. At least not as well as she liked two or three other boys at the enclave. Just because his father was a millionaire and he was tall and good-looking, Andy thought he was hell. Sally tried to be fair. Still, Andy was as frightened and worried as she was. It had been Andy who'd given her the money to take the bus to Cuernavaca while she was supposed to be staying with Conchita. Nor had he meant this to happen.

She didn't see how it could have. Andy was Tasy's boy friend and had been ever since she and her mother had moved into the community. All she'd done was to drive into Acapulco with him in search of Tasy. Hoping they might find her at Papa Juarez's, they'd dropped by The Golden Bull and had run into Conchita.

Sally stopped hugging herself and held her fevered face in her hands as she attempted, as she had a hundred times before, to reconstruct what had followed.

They'd waited for Tasy for perhaps an hour, with Conchita telling funny stories about Cuba and insisting on buying her and Andy two green coconuts apiece. She certainly hadn't been drunk. There wasn't that much gin in the coconut milk shakes that Papa Juarez served.

It had been on their way home "it" had happened. Because his own sports car was in the shop, Andy had been driving one of his father's cars. About five miles from the enclave he'd driven the car off the road and into a small clearing where some of the kids frequently parked. After he'd turned off the motor he'd sat looking at her with a different sort of look in his eyes. Then, breathing hard, he'd asked her:

"Do you feel funny, Sally?"

"Yes," she'd admitted. "I do."

"Like how?"

At first, with Tasy being her best friend, and Tasy and Andy going steady, and her not really being attracted to him that way, she'd been too embarrassed to tell him. But Andy had persisted.

"Like how?" he'd demanded to know.

Sally rocked back and forth on the bunk. And what had followed had been every bit as much her fault as Andy's. She'd been out with other boys. She had discussed the subject with Tasy and Brunnhilde and her mother. She'd known all the biological facts. But she hadn't been able to help herself. Her need had been so great she hadn't been able to deny it.

"Like I want you to love me," she'd told him.

And he had.

It had been beautiful, disgusting, revolting. And for some reason, the more times they'd made love the greater their need of each other had been. It had been like trying to put out a roaring fire with the water trickling from the spout of a tea kettle.

Most of it was still a blur. All that she really remembered clearly was that it had been hours later before either of them had been able to think coherently again. Then Andy had been saying:

"For Christ's sake, Sally, I sure hope you're on pills. Because if you aren't we can be in one hell of a jam."

Sally felt through the dark for the package of cigarettes that Charlie Lee had left her. And of course she hadn't been. Some of the girls took B.C. pills regularly. But she never had. She'd never had any reason to take them.

Now if her father found out what she and Andy had done, found out that he'd gotten her pregnant, he would kill both of them.

She found the book of matches and lit a cigarette. She still didn't understand how it *could* have happened. At least a dozen times during the last three months, since she'd known she was pregnant, trying to prove to each other that what they'd done had happened because they were so much in love with each other, they'd sneaked away from the gang and made love.

But it had never been the same as it had been the first time. They'd just been a boy and a girl on the back seat of a car, or on the beach, with her very self-conscious and embarrassed about the whole thing, afraid someone would hear or see them, and Andy not much more enthusiastic than she was.

For the last several weeks they'd even given up that. Now all they did was sit and talk about how worried they were and what they were going to do if she couldn't get rid of the "thing."

Because she hadn't dared tell anyone else and she'd felt she could trust her, she'd asked Conchita de Bravo to help them. And when the injections Conchita had suggested hadn't worked, it had been the Cuban woman's idea that they confide in Charlie Lee. "Charlie knows all the angles," she'd told her.

Now she wasn't certain this new scheme her father's bodyguard had dreamed up would work. The more she thought about it the more it sounded like the plot of one of Tasy's mother's old B pictures. It was, though, better than no plan at all. In another month the baby would begin to show. She couldn't do that to her parents. She couldn't bring that shame on her father.

Even if her father had defected from the party, he was still Chinese. He believed that a man's family honor was the most important thing in his life. If he ever found out what had happened, after he'd shot her and Andy, he'd probably put the muzzle of his gun in his own mouth and pull the trigger.

This way, if the plan worked, no one need ever know what happened.

The cramps and the ants were growing stronger, more curious every moment. It was difficult for the girl to think coherently. She forced herself to review the main details of the plan Charlie Lee had outlined to her.

That had been after he'd given her the injection she'd needed and she'd allowed him to be intimate with her, while they'd been lying on the couch in the unlighted lounge, with him squeezing and kissing her breasts and handling her, trying to get himself excited enough to take her a second time.

"No. Please, Charlie," she'd begged him. "I let you do it once, don't make me do it again."

"Why not?"

"Because you're so big you hurt me. Besides, I don't want to be cheap. I don't know why I was with Andy."

Sally wiped her eyes with the sheet again. But he hadn't paid any attention to her. He'd kept right on with what he was doing and said fiercely, "That's a fine way to talk to me, after all the risks I'm taking for you. Who the hell do you think you are, you stupid little Chinese muff? Now stop fighting and listen. Okay. So none of the doctors Conchita sent you to would abort you. I know a doctor who will. Right here in Acapulco."

She'd had to know. "You're sure?"

"I'm positive," he'd said.

Then he'd rolled her over on her back and taken her the second time, and kept right on talking while he'd hurt her.

"You see, I've already talked to the guy. But these things take time, they're tricky. So, after he aborts you, the doctor insists on keeping you under observation for forty-eight hours. That means we'll have to get you out of here for a few days. But I've figured a way to handle that.

"We both know the general defected from the party, taking a bundle with him when he left. We also know, sooner or later, they're going to try to catch up with him. So here's what we're going to do. After the operation, as soon as the doctor is certain everything is going to be all right, I'll pick you up and drive you up into the hills near some house with a telephone. And you're going to walk to the house and tell the people you were kidnapped and ask them to let you call the police. And when the Acapulco police arrive, this is what you're going to tell them."

Sally parroted the story she was to tell the police. "I was restless. I couldn't sleep. So I walked down to the clubhouse and two men I'd never seen before grabbed me and asked me if I was General Huang Ti's daughter. And when I said I was, they said the party had sent them to show the big Manchu son-of-a-bitch what it thought of defectors. Then they carried me into the lounge and stripped off my clothes and raped me."

"That," Charlie Lee said, "will explain why you're no longer a virgin and also take the heat off the young punk who got you this way. Then you'll tell the police that after both men had raped you they took you in a car to a shack up in the hills where they kept you a prisoner while they contacted your father and demanded a big ransom for your safe return. But before they could make the deal, you escaped. And your father will be so happy to see you alive and well he won't question anything you tell him."

Sally resumed her rocking. She hoped Charlie Lee's reasoning was sound. The story sounded pretty incredible to her. Still, she supposed, such a thing could happen.

She was racked by a sudden wave of nausea and tried to vomit in the metal basin but all that came up was dry phlegm. She wished they'd never left China. She wished they were still living in Hangchow. Neither her mother nor her father had liked it, but she had.

She could remember with pleasure being a member of a Happy Days kindergarten class playing elephants, marching trunk to tail, holding on to each other's hands as they'd toured the former Imperial Pleasure Gardens with their uniformed teacher patiently explaining to their little minds how much Father Mao Tse-tung loved them all and what privileged children they were to live in a droneless socialistic society of happy busy bee workers.

Then, in her pre-teens, how proud she'd been when her school girls' society had been selected to travel all the way to Peking to take part in a spontaneous demonstration, she one of thousands of girls wearing identical short blue dresses and white ballet slippers while several hundred older girls had formed a giant pyramid topped by a big red flag. Later that same night they'd all stood in Tiananmen Square and cheered when their leaders told them to and oohed and aahed over the fireworks display.

What was wrong with being one of many, of having one's life well directed? A mess like the one she was in couldn't have happened in Red China. All her father's defection had done for her was get her laid and pregnant by a boy with whom she wasn't in love; then—there was no other word for it—fucked by one of her father's own bodyguards, twice on the couch in the lounge and once after he'd brought her here. And knowing men as she was beginning to know them, even as sick as she was and as raw and sore as she was down there, Charlie Lee would undoubtedly insist on laying her again before he took her to the doctor.

After all, in her condition, what difference did it make?

She heard what sounded like the prow of a small boat nose against the lee side of the ketch and found the capris she'd discarded. She held them in front of her as she opened the door of the cabin and called, plaintively, "Charlie?"

There was a click of high heels on the companionway stairs and a moment later Señorita de Bravo turned on the light in the main cabin and said cheerfully, "I'm sorry to disappoint you, honey, but Colonel Lee is rather busy at the moment. Is there anything I can do for our little mother to be?"

"I'm sick," Sally said. "Awfully sick."

The nurse studied her with clinical interest. "Do you feel as if there were ants crawling all over and inside you?"

"That's exactly the way I feel."

"Plus cramps and nausea?"

"Yes."

"Did you try to throw up and couldn't?"

"Yes."

"Good," the nurse said. "You're coming along just fine."

Sally leaned limply against the bulkhead. "Well, don't just stand there. Do something. Do all women feel this way when they're going to have babies?"

The nurse smiled thinly as she took a small medical kit from her raffia purse and filled a hypodermic syringe with a prepared solution encased in an ampule. "You know, if I wasn't seeing this with my own eyes I would never believe it. You are a little Miss Innocent, aren't you? You still haven't wised up."

"To what?" Sally was puzzled.

"Well, for one thing, we deliberately got you pregnant."

"Oh, no."

"Oh, yes. We arranged things so it was practically a certainty. Just by mixing a healthy dose of good old-fashioned capitalistic Spanish fly in those gin and coconut milk shakes I fed you and young Carlson." Conchita added with mock solicitude, "But you never did tell me, honey. How far from town did young Carlson drive before he stopped the car and just had to put something into you? And you couldn't wait till he did?"

Sally backed away from her, sidling crabwise along the bulkhead. "Who are you? What's in that needle? What are you and Charlie Lee doing to me?"

The nurse made sure there were no air bubbles in the unit. "I think you know who we are. This is heroin in the needle, baby, and as far as Colonel Lee jumping you a few times, be grateful for the experience, because when you leave here your father isn't going to be able to help you. And peddling that pretty lemon-colored butt of yours to horny *turistas* and local playboys with a taste for Chinese tail is going to be the only way you can possibly support your baby and your habit."

"What are you doing to me?" Sally repeated.

"Have done," the nurse said pleasantly. "Our orders were to make a first-class junkie broad out of the beloved daughter of the Honorable Huang Ti. And once Colonel Lee and I figured out a way to get you to hold still for the needle, you've been very cooperative. You got on the mainline right away."

Chapter Nine

Ti had established the connection shortly after his arrival in Acapulco. If any of his pre-arranged shipments from the Orient were late or confiscated enroute, it was essential that he have access to a chemist. Thus he could always buy opium on the open market, then have his chemist refine it for sale at whatever the current market would bring. The fluctuation in the price was directly linked to the success of the Federal troops raiding and destroying the poppy fields in the more remote sections of Sonora and Sinola.

It was, in a way, a continuation of the war he'd known most of his adult life. He'd heard it estimated and he believed the report that at least one Mexican *federale* or undercover agent was killed for every illicit grower arrested. But with the profits, real and potential, being what they were, Ti had also heard that between five and six million dollars a year changed hands on a single street corner in Harlem. It was a battle without end.

"You are certain now?" he asked the man.

"I'm positive," the chemist said.

He indicated the dried stains on the pink embroidered panties. "These are definitely seminal smears, not more than eighteen to twenty hours old. As you can see they are well distributed over the garment, indicative of the purpose for which it was last used. I found identical stains on the cushion." He tapped the slide in his microscope with the glass rod in his hand. "And as I have shown you under high dry magnification, this cross section of one of the hairs I found on the garment and the cushion is the black, coarse medullated hair of a Mongolian male, indubitably pubic in origin."

"Mongolian?"

"Yes. American Indians are Mongolian. Most Mexicans are basically Indian. They and the Chinese and other Asiatics fall into the same category. The shaft of the hair is deeply pigmented and the granules of pigment are arranged with the greatest concentration just under the periphery of the cortex."

"I'll take your word," Ti said. "Now, how about the knife? Were you able to find any traces of blood that might have survived submergence in water?"

"None. But I can tell you the various colors of oil paint of which I did find traces."

Ti wrapped the knife in his handkerchief and put it in the inside breast pocket of his white linen suit coat. "That won't be necessary."

"Will you want a typed report on this, General?"

"No. Not on this," Ti said.

It was General Ti's personal opinion—and he had stated it in committee meetings and from the floor of numerous caucuses and conventions held in the Great Hall of the People in Peking—that the innate Chinese lust for life and individual gain, plus the destruction of the sanctity of the family, which had for four millennia been the lime allowing China to survive countless foreign invasions of her land, were the prime factors in the abject failure of the various agricultural and industrial "reforms" that had been foisted on the masses.

Unfortunately, however heroic they had been in their more youthful days, China's current leaders were growing old and static. They'd forgotten that when you pricked a Chinese he bled. When you tickled him he laughed. When he had carnal knowledge of a woman he wanted more. If you wronged him he wanted revenge.

Ti took the ground-down palette knife from his pocket and used the point to puncture a cigar. Then he tossed the knife on his desk and resumed his contemplation of the street outside his window as he waited for Harry Toy and Charlie Lee to return with Mr. Harris.

The narrow street was crowded with tourists and locals. The velvet-soft night was filled with the blare of brass instruments and the tinkle of pianos. In front of the nightclub up the street two naked girls outlined in neon tubing were performing the gyrations promising delights peculiar to the first two senses while a uniformed doorman standing under the sign made sure the passing *turistas* fully realized all the pleasures that could be theirs inside the club by making a universal obscene gesture.

His decision to defect hadn't been a thing of the moment. He'd been considering it for years. It had been finalized the night that Sally, twelve years old at the time, had taken part in the opening of the two-week-long national sports show in the huge Peking Workers' Stadium.

He would never forget viewing her chubby little body and earnest face grim with concentration as she'd stood on the playing field, a blob of blue in a sea of blue, intent on swinging her twin scarlet globes in absolute unison with those of the thousand other pre-teenaged girls, equally as earnest, who had participated in the demonstration. Being one of many, melding with the anonymity of her background had been to her the most important thing in her world.

And later that night, after the usual long speeches and fireworks display which he, as a party official had witnessed from the balcony of the Gate of Heavenly Peace, when he and Olga had talked to her, she'd boasted:

"I didn't make one wrong move. I did just what the girls on both sides and in front and in back of me did. Right at the same time they did it." She'd been even more pleased with herself when she'd told them, "Then when the speeches began we didn't have to think. Our group leader told us just when to cheer for Father Mao Tse-tung and when to wave our flags when Premier Chou En-lai spoke."

General Ti took his cigar from his lips and passed his palm over his mouth. This from the daughter of a house that had given China some of her greatest statesmen and literary and military men.

For that reason, he, himself, had always been suspect. His family background had kept him from getting any number of lucrative commands and finally he was shunted to a desk job in Hangchow. In modern Red China old soldiers didn't "fade away." They were drowned in the paper work of unimportant administrative posts.

Ti returned his cigar to his mouth as he considered the chemist's report. Now his Sally was out there somewhere in the night, raped or seduced and maybe dead. He had no way of knowing. He did know, now, that the party was behind this. It was their way of being clever. They were striking back at him by attacking his most vulnerable salient. He also knew that, whatever the other ramifications, the "Mongolian male" involved had to be either Harry Toy or Charlie Lee. His immediate problem was: which one?

He sat behind his desk and studied the dossiers

he'd compiled on both men before taking them into his employ. According to Harry Toy's file he'd been born in San Francisco of second-generation Chinese parents. He'd served two terms in prison, one on a state narcotics violation and one for felonious assault with intent to commit murder. The local contact and bag man for the syndicate with whom he did most of his business had vouched for both Toy's criminal record and loyalty. Toy knew only a few words of Chinese, most of them lewd or profane, but he spoke English and Spanish fluently. At the current time he wasn't wanted anywhere.

Charlie Lee's dossier was more impressive. He claimed to have been born in Paris and have a lengthy Interpol record, being currently wanted in both Marrakech and Marseilles. He said he couldn't speak any Chinese but he did speak flawless English and acceptable *pochismo,* the bastard combination of English and Spanish used mostly in border towns.

Neither man's record proved anything. Both could have been faked or compounded for just such a purpose.

Ti spun the knife on his blotter and watched the spinning blade stop with its dagger-like tip pointing toward the closed door. It had been a long day. He was tired. Once Harry Toy and Charlie Lee had determined that neither the lagoon nor the marina concealed a weighted body, he had spent most of the afternoon asking questions. He'd talked to Tasy and her mother. He'd talked to Señor Córdoba. He'd questioned Dr. and Mrs. Wilder, Colonel and Mrs. Amapa and old Mr. and Mrs. Merriwell. He'd talked to everyone who would talk to him. But mostly he'd talked to the boys and girls in Sally's age bracket. And what he'd learned had been very informative, especially the fact that, out of loyalty to her friend, Tasy had lied when he'd asked her if Sally had any special boy friend.

"No. No boy in particular," the red-haired girl had told him. "You see mostly we double- or triple-date without paying too much attention to who we're with."

However, the other teenagers had admitted that for the past three months his daughter and the tall and handsome young Carlson had been almost inseparable.

Both Harry Toy and Charlie Lee and his own instinct had insisted he question the youth immediately. He'd tried but hadn't pressed the point when Carlson's mother had told him that her son was so worried about Sally that he'd become hopelessly intoxicated. She'd asked him to postpone his questioning until the boy's father could be present.

Now that he was thinking clearly again, Ti was glad he'd agreed. The more deeply he dug into this affair the more it was beginning to take on the fine polish of a party resolution reading: "Let's make an example of Ti."

He returned to the window and stood with one foot on the sill. While he'd still been in good standing with the executive committee, he'd sat in on a number of such matters. If the script followed its usual pattern, during the next few hours more angles would be uncovered, more arrows would be aimed at some guilty intimacy between his missing daughter and young Carlson or, because the party always liked to have several strings to its bow, possibly Mr. Harris.

This would continue up to his carefully calculated breaking point. Then, with his daughter still missing, or her violated body discovered, one final weight would be thrown on the scale.

Ti flicked the ash from his cigar as he mentally

followed the ensuing sequence of events to their logical conclusion. He was known to have a violent temper and a very un-Communistic regard for the sanctity of the family. It was natural to assume that in his parental grief and sense of outrage he would attempt to kill the man responsible for whatever had happened to his daughter. That would bring the police into the case and the subsequent investigation was almost certain to reveal his trafficking in narcotics. And that would result in the confiscation of all his tangible assets and his deportation as an undesirable alien, leaving Olga and Sally—assuming his daughter was still alive—to fend for themselves in a strange country.

Or, if he killed the man, conviction of a capital crime would mean facing a firing squad or imprisonment in a Federal penitentiary for an indeterminate period of years, again unable to provide for his daughter and his wife.

Heads he lost. Tails the party won. Either way the tile fell, some smug clerk in the office of the Disciplinary Council in Peking would be able to stamp "CLOSED" on his file.

Ti rolled his cigar between his lips. Either Harry Toy or Charlie Lee could be the agent provocateur who had been sent to humiliate, then destroy him. He inclined toward Charlie Lee. Lee was too vocal in his praise of Free China, too eager to blame the mainland Chinese for everything unpleasant that happened in Asia.

Then there was the other matter, the significance of which had escaped him at the time. That had been Lee's bitter attack on one facet of their host country's culture, the working practices in the cribs in which the local whores plied their trade. A man with an alleged international criminal record, a man allegedly born and raised in Paris, shocked by having an image of Christ's agony looking on while a prostitute serviced him?

No country had a corner on morals. In old China it had been standard practice to leave unwanted girl babies by the roadside to die or sell them to the proprietors of "Flower Boats" on which, a few years later, they were forced to eke out their short lives by receiving any unwashed coolie willing to pay a few yen to expend his seed in a half-grown girl child.

New Red China wasn't much better. During the years before he'd met and married Olga, he'd never experienced any difficulty in obtaining a girl willing, for a small fee, to satisfy his need. With or without an image of Buddha witnessing the transaction.

Ti picked the razor-sharp, stiletto-like palette knife from his desk and weighed it on one palm. The knife was crude but it had a nice balance. A man could do so many things with a knife. He could sharpen a pencil or pare an apple or slit a throat or emasculate a man who had raped his daughter. After making certain, of course, he was using it on the right man.

General Ti returned the knife to his desk before answering the knock on the door. "Yes?"

"It's Harry Toy and Charlie Lee." Toy opened the door and motioned for Harris to precede him into the office. "And we've picked up that artist from the enclave."

Harris crossed the office to Ti's desk, still carrying the brown paper-wrapped canvas of the Three Graces.

"Now, look, General Ti," he began. "I think I feel almost as bad about Sally's disappearance as you do. But I told you everything I knew this morning."

Lee spoke before his employer could. "Including the fact that you were roaming around the pool area and the clubhouse stinking drunk about the time Sally disappeared?"

Harris felt what little self-confidence he'd forced himself to feel begin to ooze. "No," he admitted.

"Why not?" General Ti asked.

"Because I didn't think it mattered."

Without warning, Lee unleashed a vicious punch that sent Harris reeling across the office and into the opposite wall. "A sixteen-year-old girl is missing. There is visible, tangible evidence that she was forced to have intercourse with some man. You were in the area at the time. And you don't think it's important."

Harris wiped blood from his mouth with one hand. "I swear I didn't touch Sally. I didn't even see her."

Toy slapped Harris as hard as he could, then kneed him in the groin. "Just to refresh your memory. Come on. Let's have it, mister. What did you do? Lead the kid on, give her the old song and dance about how beautiful she was and how the difference in your ages didn't matter?"

Harris held himself with one hand. "No," he panted. "It wasn't that way at all. I swear. There's never been anything between Sally and me but a teacher-student—"

"I'll bet." Lee punched Harris again. "Talk, you Caucasian son-of-a-bitch. What have you done with Sally?"

Lee drew back his fist to strike Harris again. General Ti said sharply, "Let the man talk, Charlie. He can't very well tell us where Sally is, if you beat him unconscious."

Harris leaned limply against the wall. "Believe me, General Ti. I don't know where Sally is. And I had nothing to do with her disappearance."

Harry Toy slapped him without heat, first with the

palm, then with the back of his hand, "Why don't you stop lying to us, Harris? We spent the afternoon asking questions. And you should hear what some of the people out at Rancho Paraíso told us. Including the fact that you and your wife have been having a knock-down drag-out for the last two months. Why? Because she found out you were cheating on her with Sally?"

"I swear," Harris protested.

Before he could continue, Lee gripped his coat lapels with one hand and sank his clenched fist brutally into Harris' stomach. "Face it, fellow. Sooner or later you're going to talk. Harry and I don't just work for the general. We think a lot of Sally. We're going to go on with this until you talk."

Writhing in agony, Harris appealed to General Ti.

"You can't believe I harmed Sally. I like her, too. She and Tasy Lane are my two favorite pupils."

His plump face bland and expressionless, the one-time general of the People's Army of China merely stared back at him.

"I'll make him talk," Toy said. "I've cracked lots harder nuts than this guy."

The stocky bodyguard brushed Lee aside and executed a series of stinging judo chops that sent Harris reeling away from the wall. The canvas he was clutching fell to the floor, the paper in which it was wrapped snagging on a corner of Ti's desk.

"Hold it, Harry." Lee picked the painting from the floor. "Let's see what we have here." He tore away the rest of the paper, revealing the three nude girls.

A moment of deep silence followed. Then Lee said, quietly, "Well, what do you know? Here we've been barking our knuckles on the guy and all the time he's been carrying proof of what we've been saying." Lee handed the painting to General Ti. "Here. Take a look at this, boss. Then if you don't want to dirty your gun on the filthy son-of-a-bitch, I'll be happy to lend you mine."

General Ti studied the painting, then looked over the canvas at Harris. "You did this, Mr. Harris? You painted my daughter this way?"

"Yes," Harris breathed. "But—but no."

"What's that supposed to mean?" Toy asked.

Harris wiped away the blood that persisted in trickling into his eyes. "Just that. I painted the three girls. I painted them in those poses. But in the original all three of them were wearing bikinis and there was nothing lewd or indecent about the picture."

"I'll bet," Lee said. He slipped his gun from his shoulder holster and offered it to his employer. "How much more proof do you need, boss?"

"In due time," General Ti said. "Whoever harmed Sally will get everything he has coming. But there is something here that rather puzzles me."

"What's that?" Harry Toy asked.

"Why any sane man guilty of raping one of the girls pictured would be stupid enough to document his guilt. Just why were you carrying this, Mr. Harris?"

"I don't suppose you'll believe the truth," Harris said, "but I wanted to show it to my wife. Mrs. Harris might know who has had recent access to my studio. Someone who might have altered the canvas."

"Ah," General Ti said. "I see. In other words you claim this is a palimpsest."

"What the hell is a palimpsest?" Toy asked.

Ti continued to study the canvas. "Technically a parchment or a tablet that has been imperfectly erased and written upon again. Or, in this instance, an altered painting."

"Come off it, boss. The guy is just putting you on to

save his skin."

"That should be easily determined."

Ti laid the canvas on his desk, took a can of lighter fluid from a drawer and squirted some of the liquid on the detailed mole painted on Brunnhilde's exposed groin. Then, after waiting a moment for the fluid to saturate the paint, he rubbed at the canvas with his breast pocket handkerchief. Both the mole and the mound of blonde pubic hair came off on the cloth, leaving the teenager more or less modestly clad in a yellow bikini bottom of the type that was uniform for most of the younger girls living in Rancho Paraíso.

"Well, what do you know?" Harry Toy said. "Maybe the guy is leveling."

"I think he is," Ti said quietly. He looked over the canvas at Lee. "Which should be a lesson to us, Charlie. If I had followed your suggestion to kill Mr. Harris, we might have made a tragic mistake. Besides, what would we have done with his body?"

Harris broke the deep silence that followed.

"What happens now?" he asked hoarsely.

General Ti squirted more lighter fluid on the canvas. "To you, nothing, Mr. Harris." He used his handkerchief on the area he'd dampened. "In fact I offer my profuse and sincere apologies for the treatment you have received." He added, "And of course, I will be happy to reimburse you for any damages you feel you may have suffered."

Harris walked stiffly to the office door and opened it. "That won't be necessary," he said. "But I'd still like to know who altered my canvas."

General Ti continued to scrub at the paint superimposed on the original painting of his daughter.

"So would I," he said.

Chapter Ten

They traveled in different social circles but Harris admired what he knew of his wife's agent. A petite brunette in her early thirties, Elsie Fillmore drank her whiskey straight, was addicted to tortoise-shell combs, full, flowered Mexican skirts, white satin tie blouses that left the top rounds of her breasts and her suntanned midriff bare, and admitted that her sole interest in art was financial.

"On the rocks all right?" she asked as he joined her in the living room.

"On the rocks will be fine," Harris said. "And thanks for the use of your bathroom and the merthiolate. But why won't you tell me where Sonia is?"

His hostess sat on a white leather ottoman facing the sofa. "Because I don't know. Because I haven't seen or heard from her since around one o'clock this afternoon when she was sitting right where you are."

Harris sat cradling his glass in both hands as he studied the woman's face, trying to decide if she was lying to him.

It was difficult to determine. Most women were skilled in dissembling, and female agents more so than most. With good reason. According to what Sonia had told him, Elsie had spent the first ten working years of her life holding down two jobs. One taking care of and deferring to an over-possessive mother, the other culminating in her rise to being a highly paid copywriter and executive in a well-known Madison Avenue advertising firm.

Her metamorphosis from career girl to an artists' representative in Acapulco had been both sudden and dramatic. Some five or six years previously, shortly after her mother died, she had flown to Acapulco to spend a two-week vacation and had so fallen in love with the town and the Mexican version of *la dolce vita* that she had resigned her position without bothering to return to New York, had opened her own agency, and for the first time in her life had begun to indulge herself in the more sensuous and fundamental pleasures accruing from being pretty and shapely and female.

On at least three occasions he and Sonia had met her in the company of the virile-looking first mate of one of the luxury cruise ships plying between Los Angeles and Acapulco. They had attended a *corrida* at which one of the better *matadores* working out of Mexico City had dedicated his final and most important *toro* to her. Currently, or at least so Sonia had told him, she was enjoying the company and attentions of a Colonel Carlos Romez of the Mexican Rurales.

"Believe me, Jim," Elsie said, "if I knew where she was, I'd tell you. Now you tell me something. Had Ti's men any reason to beat you?"

"No."

"Then why was Sonia crying? Why should she have told me you don't love her any more? Have you really been playing house with General Ti's fifteen-year-old daughter?"

"Not even General Ti believes that, Elsie. Not even after he saw the canvas."

"What canvas is this?"

Harris told her in some detail.

"Anyway," he wound up, "Ti made his boys stop pounding on me, and apologized for any inconvenience he might have caused me, and let me go. And here I am wondering if you know where I can find Sonia."

"How do you know she isn't home?"

"Because I stopped and called the enclave on my way here. Córdoba told me he hadn't seen her and that none of our windows were lighted."

"What is that supposed to mean?"

"When Sonia is home she always turns on every light in the house."

"That figures," Elsie said. She looked at Harris intently for a moment "How much do you know about your wife, Jim?"

"Not much." Harris shrugged. "Oh, I know she was born and raised in Vienna. I know she's been married twice before. Once to an older man, a family friend who offered to take care of her when her mother died. Then to the GI who brought her to this country. She wanted to tell me the whole bit when we first met, but I told her that what had happened to either of us before we met was of no consequence."

"I'm not so sure," Elsie said. "But before we go into that, tell me this, will you, Jim? If you haven't been having an affair with someone else, why have you been treating Sonia the way you have these last few months? Are you tired of her? Don't you love her?"

Harris took his still damp shirt from the hanger.

"I love her very much," he said tightly.

"Then why have you stopped having relations with her?"

"Sonia told you that?"

"Yes."

Harris put on his shirt and buttoned it. "Aren't you being rather personal?"

"Very personal. But Sonia's not just a client. We're friends. And when she was here this afternoon she told me that you don't seem to want her any more.

She said that just before she left the house you came into the bathroom while she was showering and she attempted to straighten out things between you. She said she apologized for having said or done anything that might have offended you. She even tried to excite you by ... well, anyway you brushed her hand away and called her a whore. Why, Jim?"

Harris sucked in a deep breath. He ought to cut this short, but in his loneliness and near panic, he felt impelled to unburden himself.

"All you've heard is Sonia's story," he said. "How about me? Feeling the way I do about her, I've been going through hell. And the few times we've been intimate these past months—oh, hell, Elsie, I'm afraid to try any more."

"What do you mean by that?"

"Suddenly I'm washed up that way. I'm an old man. I'm through."

"At your age? I don't believe it."

"I've even consulted a doctor."

"What did he say?"

Harris sighed. "Well, he couldn't find anything wrong organically. He thought it was all in my mind. You know. My painting gone sour, the financial bind I'm in, Sonia back to displaying her body to every hack artist who can afford to pay her modeling fee—"

"Have you discussed your—your problem with Sonia?"

"Humm. Not in detail, no."

Elsie got up from the ottoman and poured more whiskey over the melting ice in her glass.

"You men and your damned pride," she said. "It was less embarrassing for you to get drunk and pick fights with her, letting her assume you were having an affair with some other woman."

She returned to the ottoman. "But have you stopped to consider if this should prove to be a temporary condition, something you could have worked out together? Your refusing to confide in her may prove to be a lot more costly than the truth."

"Would you mind amplifying that?"

"Not at all," Elsie said. "I just don't know where to begin. As Sonia has undoubtedly told you, I got into this male and female business at a fairly advanced age. I was *intacta* and very concerned about it when I was twenty-seven. Not that I wasn't honored with the usual passes. But from as far back as I can remember I'd been taught that sex was dirty, something nice girls didn't indulge in. Leaving deep-dish psychology out of it, I know the practical reason. My mother was afraid I'd experiment and like it, that I'd go to bed with and get myself thoroughly laid by some virile young copywriter or artist and settle down in suburbia with a flock of kids and a husband I adored and not enough money."

"That's all very interesting, Elsie. But I don't see that it has anything to do with Sonia and myself."

Elsie sipped at her drink. "I'm coming to that. But before I say any more, let's go back five years, to when you and Sonia first met. You say all you really know about her background is that she was born and raised in Vienna and had been married twice before you met. Once to a middle-aged friend of the family, then to the GI who brought her to this country."

"That's about it."

"Weren't you even curious about other men she might have known?"

"Yes," Harris admitted. "I still am." He tried to explain how he felt. "But right from the start I knew that what we had and could have was more than an affair. And I didn't want anything to spoil it."

"I don't follow you."

Harris paused briefly. "Look, Elsie. I'm not entirely stupid. As beautiful and desirable and experienced as Sonia is, there had to be other men in her life besides the two husbands she told me about. And I didn't *want* to know about them. I still don't. Loving her as much as I do, as much as I did from the start, I didn't want to spend a lifetime waking up in the middle of the night and lying there thinking about other men who had possessed her, thinking about—"

"Oh, come off it, Jim. Stop playing ostrich and pull your head out of wherever you're trying to hide it. If you hope to save your marriage to Sonia, it's time you knew a few things about her—things you've forced her to keep bottled up inside herself."

Harris picked his bloodstained sports coat from the couch. "I don't want to hear anything, Elsie."

"Perhaps not," Elsie said. "But you're going to. If for no other reason than I like both of you and I think your marriage is worth saving. Let's face it, Jim, Sonia has a good brain, but primarily she's a simple domestic female. If conditions had been normal for her when she was a teenager, right now she'd probably be a contented *Hausfrau* in Vienna. The most important things in her life would be getting the *Kinder* off to school and baking a *Sachertorte* for supper.

"But things weren't normal for her. When she was fifteen, just to survive, she was forced to marry a man three times her age, an old man who was fool enough to play hero and get himself shot. Leaving her scared and hungry and cold, with only one thing she could sell."

"Please, Elsie—"

"So when she got cold and hungry and frightened

enough, Sonia did just that. To a young American GI. For the first meal she'd had in three days, what amounted to a dollar and sixty cents in our money, and what was almost equally as important to her, a bar of soap."

Harris put his head in his hands. "Oh, Jesus."

"He wasn't there that night," Elsie said. "Just the American GI. I won't go into detail about what happened after that. But I do think you should know about Staff Sergeant Stephen A. Milancz."

"Who? Oh, Steve, the second—"

"Yes. The GI she married to get out of Vienna. He was glib, sly, everything most women despise in a man. Sonia said her flesh crawled every time he touched her. But he was also the key she hoped would unlock the trap she'd gotten into. Steve said he loved her. He wanted to marry her. He wanted to give her his name. He wanted to take her to the United States where no one was ever cold or poor or hungry."

"So she married the guy," Harris said harshly. "She had to—"

"That's right, Jim, a few days before he was due to be rotated, and after he'd fast-talked her into letting him take care of the few dollars she'd managed to save, she married him."

Elsie put a cigarette in her mouth and waited for Harris to light it.

"They flew to the States on separate flights, Jim. Steve left a few days before she did. And what do you think happened on her first night in New York, on what was technically still her honeymoon? Steve met her at the airport in an expensive new car. And after they'd had dinner at Lindy's he took her to their room in one of the better hotels. And, keyed up as she was by the flight from Vienna, and with everything so new and wonderful and exciting, she didn't protest when Steve insisted on claiming his rights almost before he'd closed the door of their room. After all, he was her husband, and perhaps eagerness made him brutal.

"But later Sonia began to wonder how they could afford such luxury on a sergeant's pay. And Steve told her. He'd used the money she'd given him to make the down payment on the car—and from there on out earning the family living would be up to her. You see, before he got caught in the draft, he'd been a pimp with four girls hustling for him. And he'd known that if he could get her to the States he'd have a walking gold mine."

Harris nodded. His mouth was too dry for speech.

"No more cheap stuff," Elsie said. "No more forty-schilling tricks in a cubbyhole of a room over a bombed-out antique shop. From now on, Steve told his bride, it would be a minimum of fifty dollars a date, two hundred dollars an all-night job and whatever the traffic would bear if the customer insisted on any 'special' services.

"He'd even taken some color pictures of her in Vienna, pictures she hadn't known he'd taken, and he'd used them to line up a series of dates. Her first date, an all-night job, was scheduled to start in half an hour with an oil man from Oklahoma who had a suite in the same hotel. And, Steve said if she really tried to please the guy, he might give her a bonus."

Harris sat absolutely still. Elsie shrugged.

"Well, there she was, Jim, a teenager in a strange country with no place to go and no money. She cried and begged Steve not to make her go through with it. She tried to make him understand that the only reason she'd married him was to get away from the life she'd been living. But after he slapped her around a little—being very careful not to damage the merchandise—she did the only thing she could do. She kept the date."

Elsie snuffed her cigarette. "And while Sonia didn't go into details, I guess she pleased the guy. Next morning the oil man gave her three instead of the two hundred dollars agreed upon. But when she left his suite she didn't go back to the suite where Steve was waiting for her. She pushed the down button on the elevator and took a cab to Idlewild and bought a plane ticket for Los Angeles. A few days later she got a job as a carhop in a drive-in. Then she studied modeling. She tried to better herself and eventually moved up the coast and met you."

"I remember," Harris said, "the sound of the bell—"

"She divorced Steve. She did it as soon as she'd saved enough money and lived in California long enough to establish residence." Elsie made an expressive gesture with her hands. "But that's immaterial now. You know Sonia as a passionate young woman. But she swore—and I believe her— that during the years between the morning she walked out of that hotel in New York and the afternoon she met you, she'd never stayed with a man, no matter how much he offered her.

"We both know how tough the going can get in any branch of the creative arts, and how tempted she must have been. Even now in a resort town where a man can get any woman he wants for ten *pesos* or nothing, she's a girl who could have men lined up from here to the Villa Vera Racket Club willing to pay her anything she asked if she would go to bed with them. But has she ever considered being unfaithful to you? No. Why? Because she's so in love with you she can't talk about anything else. So when things get a little rough for you and she has to go back to modeling, the only legitimate thing she knows how to do, to save what little you do have, how do you react? Instead of leveling with her and explaining your problem, you salve your male pride by playing the injured husband. You accuse her of being untrue to you with a bunch of crumbs she wouldn't spit on if China had just dropped the bomb and the whole world was on fire."

Slowly, unsteadily, Harris got to his feet.

"Well, thanks for telling me, Elsie."

"Where do you think you're going?"

"To look for Sonia. Apologize. Tell her how much I love her. Level with her."

"I don't think I'd do that," Elsie said. "If I were you I'd go home and wait for her. But while we're talking, let's see if we can't solve one of your problems. You aren't a fanatic, are you? You aren't one of those purists who think any deviation from the old masters is a desecration of art?"

"No. If I was I wouldn't be painting mail-order portraits."

"Good. In that case, let me try and see if I can't get you a few commercial assignments. And I don't mean that bust-and-buttock routine that Ahmed and Max Arnold and some of the other boys are getting rich on. Those things come and go. I'm talking about magazine-cover illustrations and car ads and things like that. After all, some of the men who are doing our leading commercial illustrations are probably getting more for painting one satisfied Cadillac owner than Michelangelo got for painting the Sistine Chapel."

Harris laughed wholeheartedly for the first time in weeks. "I doubt that. According to documented evidence, the old man got three thousand ducats or around seventy thousand dollars for that job."

"I know," Elsie said. "But he had to lie on his back to do it and it took him twenty-four years."

Harris sobered. "You'd do that for me, Elsie? Try to get me some commercial assignments?"

"Let's say for you and Sonia."

"Could you?"

"I don't see why not. You paint well, and you have a good name. I have some of the best connections in the business. I've always been a good saleswoman. While I was still with the agency, before I had any personal need for such precautions, the top brass used to boast that I was the only non-Vassar graduate, professional virgin Protestant broad copywriter on Madison Avenue who had ever succeeded in selling an appreciable quantity of B.C. pills in the more predominantly Catholic sections of the advertising spectrum. And this was before the last Ecumenical Congress."

Harris laughed again. "How did you do that?"

"It was easy," Elsie said as she walked to the door with him. "I merely suggested that joining the five to twenty-five club might be good for arthritis. Especially if a woman was between the ages of eighteen and forty and married." She wet her lips with the tip of her tongue. "Honest Injun, what did the doctor tell you, Jim?"

"Just what I told you before. That it probably was all in my mind. That if I could get rid of the mental strain and relax, things would return to normal again."

"Uh-huh. He didn't give you anything to help you physically?"

"Some vitamin shots and male hormones." Harris grinned. "But he said the best and only truly efficacious aphrodisiac is actual contact with sexy females."

"Well," Elsie said thoughtfully, "it *is* a challenging opportunity and being feminine I'm curious." Her grin was pure gamin. "But I don't think I'd better offer to play guinea pig. You are one thing Sonia has earned that I can't collect a commission on."

Chapter Eleven

After leaving Elsie Fillmore's apartment, Harris drove into the business section of the city, parked at one end of the Zocalo, and sat studying the twin blue bulbous towers of the Moorish-looking cathedral that dominated the city's central square.

At some time during his stay every artist who comes to Acapulco paints or sketches the Cathedral of Nuestra Señora de la Soledad. He'd painted it half a dozen times in different moods, subconsciously reaching out for help. No matter how sophisticated a man became, there were always times in his life when he felt somehow naked and vulnerable, once he'd lost his belief in a power greater than himself.

Still attempting to make up his mind whether to wait for Sonia at home or begin a round of the better bars and nightclubs, he turned his attention from the cathedral to the movement of the people around him.

In a good many Mexican towns, the *paseo,* the traditional courting ritual, still existed. In this ceremony the young men and young women walked in opposite directions around the local square, sizing up romantic possibilities. But Acapulco had become too large and too blasé to maintain the custom.

A few cars up the curb from where he was parked, a sharply dressed youth was talking earnestly trying to sell some romantic project or product to his girl.

The girl, not entirely convinced, but interested, was swishing her short skirt provocatively from time to time as she listened.

The girl was young. She was pretty. She radiated an aura of sex. He was amused by his own reaction as he watched her try to make up her mind. It could be he was returning to normal. He hoped so, for both his and Sonia's sake.

It wasn't pleasant for a man to learn that the woman he loved had prostituted her body, for whatever reason. But at least the attic had been swept clean of cobwebs. He hadn't learned anything that he couldn't live with.

The more he debated Elsie's suggestion, the more sensible it sounded. Like Harris himself, Sonia had a tendency to use a bottle as a crutch. She could be in any of two dozen of their former drinking places. And while he was making the rounds, she might decide to drive home and, not finding him there, become even more depressed.

He started the motor. Then, remembering that the only food he'd eaten all day had been the bowl of *pozole,* he drove to The Golden Bull. He needed a snack and he wanted to pick up that fifty dollars before he drove to the Rancho Paraíso.

The tempo of The Golden Bull had quickened. All the tables in the restaurant proper were claimed and the crowd was spilling out into the courtyard and the tables under the trees.

Juarez had gone to the jai alai games but he'd left word with the cashier to give Harris the four hundred *pesos* due him. Harris stuffed the money in his wallet and made his way between the tables to the unroofed section of the restaurant. Probably because it was more tranquil in the courtyard, there were a number of unoccupied tables. Brunnhilde and Herman were gone from the table for two but he was pleased to see Tasy sitting alone, alternately blowing up at a lock of hair that kept falling over one eye and sucking at the straw in the brown milk shake in front of her. When she saw him her face broke into a smile.

"Am I glad to see you. Papa said you might come back. Something about a check you'd cashed. And I've been sitting here waiting for hours and hours and hours."

"How come?" Harris asked as he sat across from her.

"Well, I don't have my own car and I didn't want to ride back with Herman and Brunnhilde. And I can't afford to hire a cab." Tasy was indignant. "Some dirty sneak thief stole my purse while I was in the movies." She grimaced at the milk shake before her. "I even had to cuff this. Then Papa Juarez wouldn't spring for a green one."

"That's because he knows gin isn't good for growing girls." Harris studied the menu. "But if you're hungry I'll buy you a meal before we start for home. That is, if you're not afraid to ride with me."

Tasy laid one hand on his arm. "Don't be like that, Mr. Harris. Like I told General Ti this morning, you couldn't have anything to do with whatever has happened to Sally."

"Thank you."

"You haven't heard anything about her, have you?"

"No, I haven't."

The red-haired girl leaned forward and studied his face in the flickering light of the candle stuck in a wax-covered *aguardiente* bottle. "Hey. What happened to you? Did you run into a truck or something?"

"Something like that," Harris said. He decided on

the sixteen-peso dinner featuring roast *cabrito* and gave his order to the waiter. "How about telling him to make that two dinners, Tasy?"

The girl shook her head. "No, I don't think so, Mr. Harris. For some reason I feel a little queasy. But I would appreciate it if you would buy me a drink."

"If you insist," Harris said. He added a gin milk shake to his order, waited until the waiter had gone, then said, "Juarez tells me you and Brunnhilde and Sally have been coming here often since the first time you were here with me."

"That's right," Tasy said. "Sometimes as often as two or three times a week. The prices don't take too big a bite out of our allowances and it's fun listening to the kooks. What I mean, some of them couldn't be farther out if they were on LSD. But that wasn't why we drove in this afternoon. We hoped Sally might he here."

"So Brunnhilde said. Where do you think she is, Tasy? What do you think happened back there in the clubhouse lounge?"

"I haven't any idea."

"Are you certain?"

"What do you mean by that?"

"Just that," Harris said. "And if you do know anything, I think you ought to tell either General or Mrs. Ti. Both of them are worried sick."

"Well, naturally."

Harris hesitated. "When I was here earlier this evening, I had a few words with Brunnhilde and Herman."

"Yes, they told me."

"They inferred something I'd like to discuss with you."

"Like what?"

"The possibility that Sally disappeared because she's been having a thing with one of the boys at the enclave. That he got her pregnant and she was either too ashamed or too frightened to tell her parents."

"I told General Ti this morning that—"

"I know what you told the general," Harris said. "I was there, remember? You told him Sally didn't have any special boy friend. Then when I talked to Brunnhilde this afternoon she said, 'But ever since Andy stopped holding hands with Tasy about three months ago, he and Sally have been awfully close.'"

"So sue me," Tasy said.

"Don't be like that, Tasy," Harris reproved her. "I thought we were friends. I'm merely trying to help. All I want to do is talk about it. That is, if it won't embarrass you."

"Embarrass me?" Tasy said. "This should be good. How could you possibly embarrass me? Have you ever sat around a lanai or a patio with your mother wearing a topless bikini, on the make for some good-looking young actor or second-string Mexican movie producer? Then there was the morning when we were living in the big house in Malibu and I walked out onto the lanai to get the morning paper and found her stark naked on a chaise lounge doing her morning calisthenics with the young stud who serviced the swimming pool. Go ahead. Embarrass me."

"I'm sorry," Harris said.

Tasy sipped moodily at the gin-laced coconut milk shake. "So am I. But there's nothing I can do about it for two years, when I come into the money my father left me. Then, if there's any left," she brushed her palms together, *"whish* goes little Tasy. I'll bet you don't even know my full name."

"No," Harris admitted, "I don't."

"It's Ecstasy," Tasy told him. "That's what it says on my birth certificate. And every time anyone who knows my full name uses it I feel like an orgasm." She put one of her elbows on the table and rested her chin on her hand. "All right. What do you want to talk about?"

Harris talked between bites of roast kid. "Let's start with Andy. He was drunk this morning. I asked Brunnhilde if you or the other young people had been able to sober him up before his father came home. She said you hadn't."

"No. What I mean, Andy really tied one on."

"And Brunnhilde also said that when the father did come home he was furious because Andy felt so bad about Sally's disappearance and made a remark to the effect that if something has happened to her, it's a good thing as he didn't want any part-Chinese brat in his family."

"That's what the man said."

"How do you explain that?"

"How did Brunnhilde explain it?"

"She told me to figure it out for myself."

Tasy picked up Harris' package of cigarettes and lit one in the flame of the candle. "I don't know. I don't know what to say, Mr. Harris. I don't know anything more. But I did lie to the general this morning. Until about three months ago, when Sally cut me out, Andy and I were going steady. We had been ever since mother and I moved into Rancho Paraíso."

She filled her lungs with smoke and exhaled slowly. "I don't know how to explain the way I felt about Andy." She corrected herself. "The way I feel. You see, going steady with Andy was different from anything I'd ever known before."

"How, different?" Harris asked.

"Well," Tasy said, "I don't know how it was when

you were a boy, Mr. Harris. I probably wasn't even born then. But going with a boy now is sort of like playing pro football. He tries to score and you try to stop him. And it doesn't make much difference if you're not pretty. All a girl needs to play are two goal posts and a one-yard line. And there are certain rules you play by, certain things you have to let him do and do for him, without blowing the whistle, or he won't date you. If he kicks a field goal or scores—Yeah, team, good for him. After all, you're supposed to be on pills."

Her voice filled with the wonder of the experience. "But right from the very start it wasn't that way with Andy. I didn't have to let him mess around so he'd date me. He didn't think I was plain-looking. He thought I had an interesting face. It didn't matter to Andy that mother is the way she is. He said we had our own lives to live. And two years from now, when he's twenty-one and I'm eighteen, and no one can tell us what we can and cannot do, we were going to do something about us."

"Did Andy's father object to you and Andy going steady?"

"No," Tasy said. "Both he and Mrs. Carlson sort of like me." The teenager decided she didn't like the taste of her drink or the cigarette. She pushed the milk shake away and extinguished the cigarette. "What makes it so hard for me to understand is that, in a way, it was the same way with me and Sally. She was the first real girl friend I ever had, the only one who wasn't just sucking around because my mother was in pictures and maybe I could get tickets to a sneak preview or introduce her to a star or something." She passed the tips of her fingers over her mouth in a nervous gesture. "Oh, we let Brunnhilde tag along for laughs. But it was really just Sally and me and Andy.

Then, about three months ago, it happened. I was out and she was in."

"Then Sally and Andy have been having an affair?"

"I don't know. But I do know that both of them have been avoiding me and sneaking away together whenever they get a chance." She took her fingers away from her mouth and folded her hands in her lap, fingers interlaced in an attempt to conceal their trembling. "Could we please go home now, Mr. Harris?"

"If you want to," Harris said.

He paid his bill and walked Tasy out to his car wondering if he was honor-bound to inform General Ti of what Brunnhilde and Herman had inferred and Tasy had, in part, confirmed.

As he started his car he asked, "Do you know where Sally is now, Tasy?"

"No," the girl said, "I don't. I don't even know if she's pregnant. For all I know, the way Andy acted with you this morning is just something Sally and Andy dreamed up. You know. To make their parents more sympathetic. It could be Andy has her stashed away somewhere, in a hotel or motel. Then, after a few days of everyone thinking something bad has happened to her, she'll show up again and everyone will be so relieved that neither of their parents will object when they say they're getting married."

That solution to Sally's disappearance, Harris thought, was pretty farfetched but possible. It wouldn't do any harm to wait for developments. General Ti had access to the same information he did. The way Ti was going about the affair, if Sally was in Acapulco or its environs, he'd find her. Besides, he didn't owe Ti anything. Ti had stopped his two goons from pounding on him but first he'd sent them out to bring him to his office.

As he drove down the rutted road that wound through the foothills along the coast to Paraíso Bay and La Barra de Coyuca, Harris studied what he could see of Tasy's face in the rear-vision mirror. Her affection for young Carlson seemed to be sincere. She was genuinely upset by the disruption of their relationship. She might still like Sally as a friend and be worried about what had happened to her but love was no respecter of friendship and she was still in love with Andy.

From time to time, as Tasy fought to maintain her balance in the jolting car, she used the back of a hand to scrub at her cheeks and the bridge of her nose. He felt sorry for the child. At best Tasy had a rough row to hoe. Until she got away from her mother's corroding influence, she would never have a real life of her own. Then she would always be Cara Lane's daughter.

She did, however, have two big things going for her, Harris reflected rather grimly. She was currently in the chrysalis stage of adolescence, but once the butterfly emerged she would no longer be plain. In another year, two years at the most, she was going to be more beautiful than her mother. And the other was the fact that she radiated, or perhaps "emanated" was the better word, an indefinable aura of sex.

Tasy's face might be in the formative stage, but there was nothing immature about her other feminine attributes. Her lightweight turtle-neck sweater was taut and peaked in the proper places. Sitting as she was, with feet spread and braced against the sway of the jolting car, her mini skirt crept up almost to the point of no return, and her satin-soft bare white thighs were definitely adult.

He returned his attention to the road. Minutes later the bobbing headlights of the car picked up the

"Camino Lateral" sign that marked the juncture of the private road leading down to the bay and the enclave. The windows of his house were still unlighted. When he reached it, so were those of the Lane home.

Harris got out and walked around the car and opened the door. "Conchita went into La Laja to visit her family," Tasy explained. "And when I left this afternoon Mother was talking about flying to Mexico City. She wanted to crash a house party some spick producer is giving to celebrate the start of a new picture he's just been able to finance. Who knows? If he happens to like older women he may even give her a part." As she got out of the car, she added, "Would you like to come in for a few minutes? I could make some coffee."

"No. I think not," Harris said. "Mrs. Harris should be home any time now."

"Whatever you say." Tasy smiled. "Anyway, thanks for the drink and for driving me home." She touched Harris' cheek with the tips of her fingers, then impulsively stood on her tiptoes and pressed against him, briefly, as she kissed the leathery skin her fingers had found so pleasant to touch.

"You know something?" she whispered. "You're nice. I wish just once Mother had married a man like you."

Harris watched her up the stone steps and into the unlighted house.

"It is all in your mind, *Señor*," Doctor Gonzales had said.

Elsie and the girl in the Zocalo had verified the diagnosis. And now, brief as the contact had been, Tasy had confirmed it.

He'd returned to being a normal male.

Chapter Twelve

One of the minor problems of living in Acapulco was that from the middle of December to the middle of May it seldom rained, but when it did, usually accompanied by a line squall, the wind-blown torrents of water swept in through every available opening, drenching everything within reach of its fury. The first year he and Sonia had lived in the house they'd driven into town one evening, leaving all the windows open and when they'd returned they'd found their new furnishings sodden. Now, from force of habit, no matter what season of the year it was, Harris always made sure all the windows were closed before leaving the house.

When he entered the house, he opened the windows methodically, starting in the kitchen. The beer mug and the coffee cups he and Sonia and Marcia Wilder had used that morning were still on the kitchen table. He carried the cups and the mug to the sink and rinsed them.

It would have been interesting to listen to the two women's conversation, to know what Marcia had intimated and how much of it Sonia had believed. After all, he had identified the garments and had treated Sonia badly. There had been no reason for her not to believe he could be carrying on an affair with the Chinese girl.

However, considering what Elsie had told him about her girlhood in Vienna, Sonia was in no position to throw stones. He wished now she'd insisted on confiding in him. The business in Vienna and her brief marriage to Sergeant Steve would have given him a bad time for a few days but they would have passed. Right now, it even gave him a certain sense of superiority to realize that of all the men she'd known she preferred him.

Harris walked through the house, turning on lights and opening windows as he went.

He turned on the light in the bathroom and filled the bowl with cold water. He washed his face and combed his hair.

When he returned to the living room he inspected the liquor supply. It hadn't changed. There were several *litros* of *aguardiente,* a partially filled bottle of rum he'd missed that morning, a fifth of gin and four bottles of vermouth. Good. After the acrimony of the last few months, attempting to restore their marriage to a reasonable facsimile of what it had been was going to involve a lot of talking. Even if his newly established resurgence of virility proved to be permanent, a great deal of what had to be said to eliminate all secrets was going to be embarrassing to both of them. A few drinks would help when Sonia came home. A few more bottles would help in the days ahead.

Señor Córdoba added two jiggers of lemon juice to the pink ladies he was making for Colonel and Mrs. Amapa and shook the mixture vigorously.

Ten thousand *pesos.* Plus a new house and a plot of ground of equal size farther back in the hills. That's what Señor Perusquia, the Federal man in charge of the expropriation, had offered. Back in 1946 that had seemed like a fortune. Even so, a large number of local landholders had been reluctant to make the exchange. They'd liked living on or near the bay and the life of the government man had been threatened so many times he'd been forced to post an announcement in the market stating that he would receive threats of assassination only on Tuesdays and Thursdays.

Córdoba gave his shaker an extra flourish, then strained the mixture into the glasses on Paquita's tray and began work on a frozen daiquiri and a grasshopper for Dr. and Mrs. Wilder.

Now it transpired the *paisanos* who had threatened Señor Perusquia had good reason to feel the way they did. When it could be obtained, land that had sold for ten *pesos* a square meter in 1946 was finding a ready market at ten thousand *pesos*. Once the boom had spread from Las Playas back into town and along the bay there'd been no stopping it. Acreage he could have bought for *tacos,* jumbles of rock on which not even squatters had wanted to live, was bringing sixty-five thousand dollars an acre.

Córdoba patted at the perspiration on his jowls with a clean bar towel. It made a man think. If *Dios* had put his brains where they should be, he could be a rich man. If he'd dared to gamble on rising land values, he wouldn't have to be mixing drinks for a bar full of drunks. He could be living in a mansion on Puerto Marques Bay with someone making drinks for him.

It wasn't as if he hadn't always earned good money, first as a youth diving from La Quebrada, then as assistant barman and finally head barman at El Mirador Beach Club.

But what had he done with his money? Had he invested it in land? No. He'd spent it on milk and diapers and dozens of pairs of *poco* pants and pinafores. With more girls than he could remember, even an occasional *turista,* out of their minds about him, he'd had to get between one pair of *café-con-crema*-colored thighs. And Luiza being a good girl, faithful in attendance at both mass and confession, there'd been only one way he could get there. And eight deep breaths and ninth months after Father Zamora had pronounced them *hombre* and *esposa,* the first of the babies had come. Even now, fifteen years later, with him almost forty years old and Luiza twenty-nine, it seemed that every time he hung his pants on the bed post—*Olé*. He'd won another *lotería*.

Córdoba took the signed chit from Paquita's tray and replaced it with the drinks he'd made and decided to tell Pepe to remind his young wife that when she was serving drinks she was supposed to wear her shoes and a *camisa*. Either that or keep her blouse buttoned. Olives or onions in martinis, *si*. That was a matter of personal preference. But *poco* peaked purple nipples in frozen daiquiris, no. What men looked at they wanted to touch. What they touched they wanted to use. And there was enough of that sort of business going on in Rancho Paraíso now.

With nothing to do for the moment, Córdoba studied the faces of his patrons.

Colonel and Señora Amapa, the young woman half the deposed dictator's age who posed as Señora Amapa and presumably performed all wifely functions, and Señor and Señora Anderson were playing one of their endless games of gin rummy.

At one of the two poker tables, Señor Gottlieb senior was arguing government restrictions on the current low price of silver with four other retired mining men. At the other poker table, Herr Major Klein, as he preferred to be addressed, and Capitan Serge Chernovsky, who claimed to be of Polish origin but who regularly received mailed copies of *Tass* and

Pravda, were riffling a deck of cards and stacking chips while they held a discourse on the day's military mistakes throughout the world, waiting for enough players to drop in to form a game.

Not far from them, Dr. and Señora Wilder, having nothing more to say to each other, were staring into the untouched drinks Paquita had just served them.

As far as Córdoba knew, young Carlson hadn't returned to the clubhouse since the other youngsters had walked him home that afternoon but Tasy Lane, sitting at one of the tables against the wall, was deep in earnest conversation with Señor Carlson while the bulk of the younger crowd was still cavorting in the pool or dropping coins in the jukebox on the flagging to get music to which to dance. Córdoba listened to what he could hear of the lyrics issuing from the jukebox....

Given a choice, Córdoba decided he still preferred "Estrellita."

He looked from the open door to the red leather bar stool on which Señora Ti was sitting, staring at the phone, which she'd been doing since her husband had called an hour ago.

"Thank you for your concern," she'd told him when, as delicately as he could, he'd suggested he was still of the opinion that the police should be informed about her daughter's disappearance. "But this is a family matter. As yet the general hasn't ascertained our daughter's whereabouts, but he is taking the necessary steps to assure her safe return."

Unfortunately, Córdoba thought, the installation of individual phones had been one of the things he and the developers of Rancho Paraíso had overlooked in their planning. Because of the population explosion and demand, the requirements for extended telephone service were complicated and costly. To have one installed in the bar, they'd been required to buy stock in the parent company, purchase the phone for cash, then pay their share of having the wire extended from the trunk line that serviced Coyuca de Benitez and the small fishing village a few miles up the coast.

The things a businessman had to do to earn a modest living and put away a little for his and his wife's old age. Not to mention an education for twelve children.

Now, two years after the phone had been installed, along with being an unpaid postman, he was forced to run an equally unprofitable answering service, taking messages whenever possible. When the caller insisted, he had to despatch either Juan or Pepe away from their regular duties to inform the householder that he or she was wanted on the phone.

Córdoba sighed as Harris appeared in the doorway of the bar. He liked Señor Harris. In spite of the fact that he'd heard some of the residents claim she was posing *desnudo* for other artists, he admired and respected Señora Harris. He and Luiza would always treasure the group portrait the artist had painted of their children. It was the nicest *Navidad* present they had ever received. It would always hang in a place of honor on their wall.

But neither Señor nor Señora Harris had the least conception of the value of money. He'd heard it said that all artistic people were slightly *loco*. He believed it. When the Harris couple had money, they spent it as if it grew on trees. When they had no money, they ran a tab. At present they were into him for almost two hundred dollars, U.S. Not counting the three delinquent payments on their house. As reluctant as he was to do so, if the artist wanted to extend his credit he was going to have to cut him off at the pockets until he paid a little something on account.

"I'll have the usual double," Harris said. "Plus a half dozen bottles of whiskey to go." Then before Córdoba could speak, he took his wallet from his pocket and counted twelve hundred *pesos* of the money he'd received from Papa Juarez and laid them on the bar. "Oh, and before I forget it, here's a hundred and fifty bucks on our back tab."

"Si, Señor," Córdoba beamed as he picked up the money. "One double bourbon and six bottles to go coming up."

Harris sipped at the whiskey Córdoba had set before him. Then, seeing Mrs. Ti at the end of the bar, he picked up his glass and sat on the stool next to hers.

"Is there anything new on Sally, Mrs. Ti?"

"Yes and no," the woman said. "I've just received one call from the general and I'm waiting for another. You see, he thinks he knows now who induced her to stage that little scene this morning. And as soon as he determines her exact whereabouts, he is going to phone me again and we are going to her together."

Harris studied the woman's face. He would like to paint her sometime. It was easy to see where Sally had gotten her looks. In her youth, the Russian woman, probably of Georgian or Circassian ancestry, must have been very beautiful. Now that she'd reached her forties, she was still a slim-figured, full-bosomed woman with a regal bearing that befitted her position as a general's wife. He wouldn't want to earn her enmity, though. There was a certain tilt to her head, a firmness to her chin and an unspoken but obvious disregard for the opinion of others about her that reminded him of portraits he'd seen of Russian aristocracy.

"Good," Harris said. "I'm glad to hear no serious harm has come to her. Sally is not only one of my best students, she's a well-mannered, lovely child." He stretched a point. "Mrs. Harris and I are very fond of her."

Mrs. Ti laid one of her jeweled, fine-boned hands on his forearm. "Thank you, Mr. Harris. And if there has been any misunderstanding, if you have been inconvenienced, both the general and I apologize. In turn, Sally is very fond of you. She's always spoken of you and Mrs. Harris in the warmest terms."

"I'm glad to hear that."

"Mrs. Harris is well?"

Harris temporized. "Yes. But a trifle late getting home tonight."

He looked through the mullioned picture window at the road winding up the wooded hill to his house. Even with all the windows lighted and opened it looked untenanted. Suddenly he didn't want to be alone in the accusing silence of the rooms while he waited for Sonia. From the stool on which he sat he could see the headlights of any car turning down the black topped road and easily reach the house to welcome Sonia before she could park her Toyota and climb the short flight of stone steps that led up from the patio.

He added to what he'd just said, "In fact, I'm becoming a little worried about her."

A half hour passed. An hour. Two hours. Three. He and Mrs. Ti were still waiting, she for her husband, he for Sonia to come home, when the last game had been played, the last couple had left, Juan and Pepe had begun to stack the chairs and tables and Señor Córdoba, profusely apologetic, announced he was closing for the night but he would be happy to transmit any message if either the general or Señora Harris should call.

Chapter Thirteen

The going rate was twenty-five *pesos* an hour, with the average ride lasting an hour. But, on occasion, the driver of one of the *calandrias* clustered across from the Zocalo picked up a live *turista* who engaged his horse-drawn open carriage for an unspecified length of time. Paco Gualterio Ríos had gotten himself a live one. But then, Ríos reflected as he drove, no matter what flags their ships might fly, sailors were good spenders.

Sonia liked this man. Lieutenant Commander Paul Edwards was young. He was handsome. He seemed to have an unlimited supply of money. Not once during the nine hours they'd spent in each other's company had he made one off-color or suggestive remark or behaved other than an officer and a gentleman.

Slightly high from the drinks she'd consumed, but still in possession of all her faculties, she lay relaxed and content against the white-uniformed arm between her and the musty-smelling black leather seat of the *calandria,* enjoying the clop of the horse's hoofs as the rubber-tired carriage rolled sedately along Costera Aleman.

Clop, clop past the lighted beer gardens. Clop, clop past the Dairy Creme stand selling soft ice cream. Clop, clop past the miniature golf links. Clop, clop past the romantically inclined couples strolling along the promenade.

This was the way she liked to live. This was the way she'd hoped to live. This was the way she and Jim had lived when they'd first moved to Acapulco.

"Are you having a good time?" Lieutenant Commander Edwards said.

"Wunderbar," Sonia assured him.

"And you're enjoying the ride?"

"Very much."

But Sonia's escort continued to be concerned about her. "How about the drink department? Do you want to have the driver stop somewhere? Or can you hold out until we get to the El Presidente?"

"I'm doing nicely, thank you."

Edwards tightened his arm around her shoulder and pressed the fingers on one gloved hand. "You're sure, now, you want to go to the Jacaranda Club?"

"I'm sure."

"Do you think the show is as good as they say it is?"

"That I wouldn't know," Sonia said. "But everyone to whom I've talked who's seen it says it is very colorful and exciting. You see," she explained with alcoholic gravity, "the way it's been told to me, an actor made up as an old Aztec priest puts a virgin Indian maid on an altar—anyway a girl who's supposed to be virgin—and pretends to cut out her heart."

"That sounds very colorful," Edwards said.

Sonia made herself more comfortable against his arm. "This is going on while the *volodores,* whatever that means, are climbing a pole one hundred feet high. After the sacrifice, the priest holds up the girl's heart and one man beats a small drum and dances on a little platform on top of the pole, and the rest of them jump out into space head first and whirl around and around the pole about twenty-five or thirty times before they reach the ground."

The navy man considered Sonia's statement with an alcoholic profundity as deep as hers.

"You say this pole is a hundred feet high?"

"That's what I've been told."

"Then what keeps them from breaking their necks?"

"The ropes that tie them to the pole. They used to use vines in the old days. But now they use ropes. You see it's a combination of a hundred-year-old ceremony of the—" she had trouble with the proper name and started over—"a one-hundred-year-old ceremony of the Tononac Indians that was supposed to bring rain, and an old Aztec religious rite."

"Oh," Edwards said. "I see." He lost interest in the subject. "But let's talk about us. You do like me a little, don't you, Sonia?"

Sonia returned the pressure of his fingers.

"I like you a lot. You should know that by now, Paul."

"Do you like me enough to let me kiss you?"

Sonia pretended to be shocked. "Right in the middle of Costera Aleman? What would the natives think?"

"To hell with the natives."

"Later," Sonia promised.

"Whatever you say," Edwards said. He lit two cigarettes and gave one of them to her.

"Danke," Sonia thanked him. She puffed on the cigarette thoughtfully. The next time Paul asked if he might kiss her, she'd let him. She might even kiss back. Why not? Jim didn't need or want her any more.

"And you're certain you feel all right?"

"I feel fine," Sonia said.

She rode, listening to the clop of the horse's hoofs, trying to assure herself of what she'd just said. She hoped she knew what she was doing. For a day that had started out as badly as this one had, it could become a major turning point in her life.

She reviewed it chronologically. All in all, it had been quite a day. After she'd blubbered on Elsie's shoulder and Elsie had written a check for the money due her, she'd driven directly to the bank. Then she'd stopped at the *farmacia* in the same block to buy some cosmetics and facial tissues and another bottle of seconal capsules.

She'd had every intention of keeping her appointment with Max Arnold. After all, it meant another fifty dollars. When she had returned to her car she'd even driven halfway to his studio in the hills overlooking Revolcadero Beach. Then, possibly because of the scene with Jim, the thought of standing nude on a dais with a dirty old man leering at her suddenly became abhorrent.

The hell with it, she'd thought. The hell with everything. Let the bank have the house.

So instead of keeping her appointment she'd turned her car around and driven to one of the smart shops on the Calle Hidalgo. There she'd spent most of the money Elsie had given her on the original sports creation she was wearing—the first really good outfit she had bought in six months.

Sonia tried to tug the skirt of her new dress over her knees but it was much too short. The skirt wasn't quite as revealing when she walked or just stood. But she had to be careful how she sat or very little of her underpinning was left to a viewer's imagination.

However, buying the new outfit had helped. She'd felt sufficiently *soignée* to drive to the Acapulco Hilton. I'll show Jim, she'd thought. Even if she had been one, no man, especially her husband, could call her a whore.

Then after lunch in the patio room, the swank dining room built on the small peninsula extending out into the hotel's swimming pool, during which she had tried without much success to stop crying, she had decided that what she needed was a drink. Possibly a lot of drinks.

Sonia studied the man sitting beside her through her lashes. So she had moved to the bar and that had been when Lieutenant Commander Paul Edwards of the United States Navy came into her life.

Sitting two bar stools away, he'd looked at her and said, "If I seem to be forward, *Señorita,* forgive me. But haven't we met? Haven't I seen you somewhere before?"

For a moment the old fear had come back. A number of young U.S. Navy men had been among her best customers in Vienna. By now one of them could well be a lieutenant commander.

"Oh, God. It's finally happened," she'd thought.

But it hadn't been that at all. "Of course," he'd added as he had moved to the stool beside the one on which she was sitting. "You're the model. You have to be the model for the painting I saw in Admiral Connors' rumpus room the other night. A very artistic and beautiful nude painted by someone who signed himself Abdul Ahmed. But, if I'm not being impertinent, nowhere near as beautiful as the original."

Sonia tugged at her skirt again, and smiled. She'd been so relieved that she admitted posing for Ahmed—and after that, Paul had introduced himself. He explained that he was bored and lonely and on the last day of a ten-day leave, and asked if he might buy her a drink.

"That way," he'd grinned, "when I rejoin my ship I can boast to my fellow officers that while I wasn't too impressed with Acapulco I did buy a drink for a real live model. One of the most beautiful women they or I will ever see."

Putting it the way he had, how could she refuse him? So, Sonia thought alcoholically, she'd let him buy her a drink. She'd let him buy her a lot of drinks. And from then on Acapulco was theirs.

First they'd gone for a swim in the Hilton pool, both of them slightly high, bobbing up and down in the water, with Paul saying clever things and making her laugh as she hadn't laughed in weeks, but always the perfect officer and gentleman, looking at and admiring what the bikini she always kept in her model's case revealed, but never attempting to become unduly familiar or saying anything off color.

Sonia flicked the cigarette he'd given her out of the *calandria* and turned her head to watch the bright sparks die on the pavement. That would come later. She still had to make up her mind how their day together would end.

She relaxed against the uniformed arm under her shoulders. However it might end, she'd never had a more pleasant day. After they'd finished with the Hilton pool, she and Paul had done a dozen inconsequential but interesting things that she'd always wanted to do but which she and Jim had never gotten around to doing.

They'd strolled across the Zocalo and been serenaded by a *mariachi* band. They'd explored the public market and Paul had bought her an armful of flowers, which she left on some bar along the way. They'd gone for a ride down the bay on one of the sightseeing boats catering to *turistas*. They'd ridden the ferry from Galeta Beach to La Roquetta and the view from the top of the lighthouse had been as beautiful as everyone said it was.

They'd watched the charter fishing boats come in. They'd had drinks at the Villa Vera Racket Club and, with the coming of night, drinks on the Starlight Roof of the Palacio Tropical and still more drinks on the terrace of El Mirador while they'd watched the diving boys of La Quebrada plunge 118 feet into 12 feet of water. This with a flaming torch in both hands.

Then, slightly sobered by the elaborate meal that Paul had ordered, but still restless and looking for more excitement, they'd gone to the jai alai *frontón* and Paul had won three thousand *pesos*. Now they were on their way to view the Indian pageant at the Jacaranda Club in El Presidente Hotel. What happened after that would be up to her.

Sonia felt a little sad. It seemed a pity that all the good years that she and Jim had known might end with her in another man's arms.

"Are you sure you're all right?" Edwards asked.

"Yes."

"Then why so silent?"

"I'm thinking."

"About us, I hope."

"In a way."

"Good."

Their entrance into the Jacaranda Club was in keeping with the rest of the day's activities—impressive. Lieutenant Commander Edwards hadn't bothered to make reservations, but that was of small importance. In Mexico the military still ranked only one niche lower than the gods, and once the maître d' glimpsed Edwards' white dress uniform and the scrambled gold braid on his cap there was a frenetic snapping of fingers and a scurrying of busboys and a front table was made immediately available to the officer and his *Señorita*.

The pageant was all it was advertised to be, cleverly conceived, elaborately costumed and brilliantly staged.

High as she was, perhaps because she was high, Sonia enjoyed it very much. She wept with the almost nude Aztec maiden about to be sacrificed on the stone altar, shuddered when the priest displayed what was purported to be her still throbbing, bloody heart, thrilled as the *volodores* plunged from the tiny platform on top of the tall pole and whirled around and around and around in the perilous descent that climaxed the pageant.

After the show, they had more drinks and danced. Then, back in the *calandria* again, with the horse plodding sedately along Costera Aleman and the driver looking discreetly ahead, Sonia realized that while she was still fully cognizant of what she was doing, the lights along the waterfront had grown nimbuses since she'd last seen them. Also, Paul was speaking to her.

"May I kiss you now?" he asked.

"If it would please you," she said.

As he did everything else, Lieutenant Commander Paul Edwards kissed well. Sonia liked the even pressure of his lips on hers. She enjoyed the sharp, clean scent of the after-shaving lotion he used, the preliminary sensations evoked by the muscular fingers busily kneading the bare flesh of one of her thighs, but being careful to limit their range to the area between her knee and the hem of her skirt.

"Now what?" Edwards asked as they kissed.

Sonia touched one of his smoothly shaven cheeks with her fingers. "What would you like to do, Paul?"

"You know what I want to do."

"Tell me."

"I presume you want me to be honest?"

"Yes."

"I'd like to tell the driver to drive us to my hotel,

then take you up to my suite and admire and kiss every inch of your beautiful body."

"Then make love to me. All the way, as the saying is."

"Frankly, yes."

"So that when you return to your ship you can boast to your fellow officers that while you were in Acapulco you not only bought drinks for a real live model, but went to bed with her?"

"No."

"Then why?"

"Because you're so beautiful and exciting. Because I've been that way ever since I saw you sitting on that bar stool at the Acapulco Hilton."

Sonia considered his answer. It was as good as any she'd heard and more honest than most. The decision was up to her. If she said no Paul would have the driver take them back to where they'd left her car and the adventure would be over. There would be no recriminations. Paul would be disappointed, but he wouldn't make a scene or abuse her.

That wasn't the way men in his stratum of society reacted. Their parting would be proper and formal. When they reached her car Paul would bid her a polite goodnight and tell her what a good time he'd had and how pleased he was to have spent the day in her company.

While she drove home to—what?

Her mind raced on as she lay with his arms around her, one cheek pressed to his chest, listening to the pound of his heart, savoring the sheer strength of the man, the scent of male vitality he exuded. She was still a young woman with all a young woman's passion and need for sexual fulfillment. She'd tried to be a good wife to Jim Harris. She'd never been unfaithful to him. She'd never even considered being unfaithful. But Jim didn't want or need her any more. He hadn't been a real husband to her for weeks. And when she had tried to bridge the widening gap between them, he had called her a whore.

"I'll tell you what," he'd said. "When I want to get laid or have any erotic services performed, suppose I let you know."

This to his own wife. This to the woman he had promised to love and cherish, in all faith and tenderness, as long as they both should live.

She made her decision. "All right, Paul."

"All right what?" Edwards asked.

Sonia put her hand on the fingers kneading her thigh and pressed them even more deeply into her flesh. She raised her face to be kissed.

"Let's do what you want to do, Paul. Tell the driver to take us to your hotel."

BOOK THREE

While Acapulco has always been a popular resort with Mexicans, its phenomenal growth during the past twenty-five years, plus the attendant adjustment of expansion, plus the fact the majority of its permanent residents earn their livelihood from some form of tourism, has created certain problems common to all large municipalities that are subject to seasonal influxes of free-spending non-nationals. One of the most pertinent, true in all resort cities, is that while the directors of the local branch of the Consejo National de Turismo *insist on a proper maintenance of law and order, it is wary of any enforcement that is too strict, or any police harassment apt to ruffle the plumage or frighten away the flocks of golden geese seeking* la dolce vita *and laying so many shining golden eggs on the equally shining golden sands of this tropical toehold on Paradise.*

Chapter Fourteen

Blanca Berrios was a deeply religious woman. She was also one of the human river of unskilled hotel workers and house maids living in La Laja, the eighty-six-acre community of eight thousand squatters, who flow down through the hills every morning to the hotels and private homes in which they are employed.

This morning she paused in front of the crude wooden cross that the *padre* who managed the Casa Hogar de Nino had erected in front of the small chapel serving the spiritual needs of his orphans to make the sign of her faith and say an act of contrition.

She doubted that the good *padre* would approve of her working in a *casa* as morally lax as that of Señor Ahmed's. There'd been a time when she would have worried about her own virtue. But now she was forty and fat and even her husband no longer evinced much interest in what few charms she still possessed so she didn't think she was in any danger of being forced to submit to an act worthy of the confessional.

All Señor Ahmed wanted from her was a clean house, *desayuno* served for *uno* or *dos* as the case might be, tasty noon and evening meals and a certain amount of discretion.

Blanca continued on down the hill with her early-rising fellow workers. It was a difficult sensation to explain but for some reason she had a feeling this would be a good day, that something nice was going to happen to her. But then, it could be because it was the end of the month and sometime during the next few hours Señor Ahmed would place in her hands the one hundred and ninety-two *pesos* she had earned.

The impressive *casa* overlooking the bay was still cloaked in sleep and silence when she reached it. Knowing just when Señor Ahmed would awaken and whether he would want breakfast for one or two was always one of her problems. Either way, Blanca decided, she would serve the compote of papaya, pineapple, tangerines and bananas she'd made the afternoon before, *huevos y tocino,* crusty hot *bolillos* with strawberry jam and of course *café con crema.* There was nothing like bacon and eggs to put a man in a good mood and the chilled compote would settle his stomach if her employer had overindulged.

She filled a coffee pot with water, spooned the proper amount of coffee into it and set it on the stove. She turned on the oven so it would be ready for warming the rolls. She took the eggs and the bacon from the refrigerator and made sure the compote had chilled properly. Then her preliminary preparations completed, she climbed the stairs to the upper hall to peer into the master bedroom and determine, when Señor Ahmed did ring, whether he would want one or two trays.

There was no one in the bedroom. The ornate spread on the bed hadn't been removed. It was as taut and unrumpled as it had been when she'd finished changing the linen the morning before. Nor had Señor Ahmed said anything about going away.

Puzzled, the woman continued on down the hall to the studio to see if, as he infrequently did, her employer had become so interested in what he was painting or had such a rush of orders that he'd worked all night.

The high-ceilinged studio was as devoid of life as the master bedroom. The heavy drapes on the huge window that framed a large section of the city and bay were still undrawn against the morning sun that faded everything on which it shone. Even more important, while Señor Ahmed had given strict orders that no one was ever to touch any of his pictures, someone had disturbed the canvas on which he was currently working. One corner had slipped off the easel and was resting on the *plataforma* where the models who posed for him stood.

Blanca was hesitant to enter the room without permission. Since the first week, three months before, when she'd begun working for Señor Ahmed, whenever it did not conflict with her duties, she'd made a point of staying out of the studio. She'd learned that any unannounced intrusion could be embarrassing. Her employer not only earned his living painting *desnuda* young women, he frequently made upon them demands other than posing.

She found this out the second day she'd come to work for him. She'd walked into the studio to inform him that the ancient *enfriadera* in the kitchen would no longer make ice cubes, nor would it keep anything cold, and found him kneeling in front of one of his models with the girl standing spread-legged to receive his attentions, the golden tassel of his red fez bobbing like a turkey's wattle and the girl's neck arched and her lips drawn away from her teeth, in *éxtasis* at the sensations the kneeling man was evoking in her.

That same night, curious, in the privacy of their bedroom, after she'd told her husband what she'd seen she'd asked him, "Why don't you ever make love to me that way?"

And Guido had said, "You say this girl was young?"

"*Si.* Not more than sixteen."

"But fat and lumpy with big, dangling bosoms?"

"No. She had a slim and very beautiful body with pert little pink-tipped breasts."

And Guido had sighed and told her, "All right. I tell you what. The next time you are sixteen and have a beautiful body and little pink-tipped breasts, remind me and we will discuss the matter again."

"Señor Ahmed," the housekeeper called.

She called a second time. When her employer failed to answer she entered the studio to draw the drapes and straighten the canvas. Instead she clapped the back of one hand to her mouth.

Señor Ahmed would be furious when he saw what had happened to his painting. The last time she'd seen the picture it had been a life-size reproduction of a firm-breasted young girl wearing a pair of filmy green pants that did not conceal but drew attention to her sparsely haired rojo-colored center piece.

But since she'd last seen the canvas someone had slashed the model's face beyond recognition. Then, not content with that, the vandal had cut a heart shaped hole where the girl's symbol of femininity had been.

Blanca felt as if a cold hand were squeezing her bowels. All the good feeling she'd experienced that morning left her. This wasn't going to be a good day, after all. She turned her attention from the mutilated painting to the studio. Nothing but the picture had been vandalized. None of the other canvasses had been touched. The chairs were all in their proper places. The brushes were still in their jars. The palette he'd been using was on his work table.

A faint, clicking sound intruded on her consciousness. The housekeeper tried to identify it, then realized what it was. Either Ahmed or one of the girls who posed for him had failed to shut off the record player in the small room adjoining the studio where the models dressed and undressed.

She walked to the door of the room to shut off the machine and again clapped her hand to her mouth.

Alive, Señor Ahmed had presented an impressive, even handsome appearance. He'd been *muy caballero*. Now, lying as he was on the floor of the small room, his flabby belly and fat genitals bulging out of a pair of unbuttoned yellow polka-dot shorts, his red fez fallen from his bald head and his sightless eyes attempting to peer under a rumpled bed that would be of no more use to him, all the artist looked was— Blanca searched for a word to describe it, and found one. All Señor Ahmed looked was *cómico*. She'd never seen anything more ludicrous-looking.

She watched with morbid curiosity as a buzzing

blue bottle fly left the bloody area on the back of her late employer's head, circled the room and landed tentatively on the dead man's exposed manhood.

"Ding-a-ling-a-ling, he was a big one," she thought. "No wonder I had to serve *desayuno* for two so many times."

She felt a little sad. Alas. All that was over now. This was a matter for the *policia*. She would have to inform them immediately that her employer was dead, Blanca thought, by the same hand that had mutilated the painting in the other room. The police would ask her ten thousand personal questions:

Do you know the names of any of the girls who posed for him? With how many of them did he have intimate relations? Do you know any father, husband, lover, brother who ever threatened his life? Describe some of these girls?

Not that what she could tell them would be of much help. With the exception of the blonde Señora who'd always been very gracious to her and the red-haired girl child she'd seen on the second day she'd come to work, she doubted if she would recognize any of Ahmed's models, with or without their clothes. The girls had come and gone without introducing themselves to her or confiding their family or marital status. All any of them had been to her were briefly seen figures in the front doorway or a second face in the king-size bed in the master bedroom on the mornings when she'd been required to serve two breakfast trays. Even then, in belated modesty, most of the little sluts had kept their faces averted.

The housekeeper started to leave the doorway to call the police and remained to glower at the man on the floor.

Now Señor Ahmed was dead, who was going to pay

her the one hundred and ninety-two *pesos* she had coming? Money for which she had cooked and scrubbed and dusted and shopped and put up with an ancient stove and a wheezing refrigerator that should have been replaced years before.

She doubted that there was any money in Señor Ahmed's wallet. For fear of being robbed or of having his pockets picked, her late employer had seldom carried any money on his person. He'd paid all the household bills, including her wages, by check, used credit cards to purchase his personal things and signed tabs for his meals when he dined out. Besides, now he was dead, she didn't believe she could bring herself to touch anything that belonged to him, nor did she want to do or touch anything that might lead the police to suspect she had something to do with his death.

The incessant buzzing of the fly and persistent click of the needle in a deeply scored groove of the expended record annoyed her. There was nothing she could do about the fly. She could shut off the machine.

She turned off the record player and it was then that she saw the purse, one of the small clutch kind that some young women affected. The housekeeper picked it up and opened it. All it contained was the usual trivia found in most women's purses, a lipstick, an eyebrow pencil, some bobby pins, a small change purse containing twenty centavos, two *norteamericano* dimes, one Juan Kennedy half dollar, two folded ten-peso notes and a shopping list written on the back of an old envelope.

Blanca's eyes turned cunning. The purse hadn't been in the room when she'd cleaned yesterday. That meant the girl to whom it belonged could be involved in Ahmed's death. It could have been her husband or lover who had killed Señor Ahmed, then mutilated the painting of her to keep her from becoming involved.

The housekeeper put the purse in the pocket of her apron and retraced her steps to the kitchen. There she drank a cup of coffee while she went through the contents of the purse a second time.

She didn't want to get anyone in trouble. She couldn't care less about Señor Ahmed. He was so much burro dirt. As Father Martinez had said during his sermon several Sundays before, men who lived by the sword died by the sword and Señor Ahmed had died by his.

But what she had in mind wouldn't be much to ask. Even if the girl who owned the purse wasn't involved in the nasty business upstairs, she should be grateful. In exchange for keeping her name out of it, the girl should be grateful enough to pay Blanca the money due her. It was even possible she might give her a few additional *pesos*.

Blanca turned the envelope over. It bore the business name of an Acapulco dress shop that catered to *turistas* and other wealthy non-nationals and was addressed to:

> Señora Cara Lane
> Rancho Paraíso
> GPO
> Acapulco

Blanca was indignant as she spooned more sugar into her coffee. If he had to plunge his *espada* into one too many tender scabbards, the least her late employer could have done was to make out a check for her wages before he got himself killed.

Twenty-four dollars, U.S., was a lot of money. It would feed and house her children for a month.

Chapter Fifteen

Tuesday morning dawned hot and clear with no trace of clouds in the sky. With two exceptions there was nothing to distinguish it from a hundred other mornings to which Harris had awakened since he and Sonia had moved to Paraíso Bay.

One of the exceptions was that he awakened sober, completely sober, for the first time in weeks. The other was that it was the first time he realized a man could miss anyone so much. If Sonia's failure to come home last night wasn't merely a retaliatory measure, if this was the beginning of a permanent separation, he didn't know what he would do. That prospect was too unpleasant to contemplate.

It had been four o'clock before he'd even tried to sleep. Then for the next two hours he'd sprawled in a state of suspended animation, hoping every minute to hear her Toyota turn into the carport, or hear Señora Córdoba bang on the door and tell him that Sonia had just phoned and said she was sorry but she'd had too much to drink and she thought she'd better not drive and would he please come into town and get her.

That was the way it happened in books. But that wasn't the way it had been for him. He'd just stayed awake and sweated.

Harris looked at his watch and was surprised to see it was a few minutes after nine. He must have dropped off to sleep shortly before daybreak.

He got up from the easy chair in the living room in which he'd fallen asleep and stared through the sliding screen door. It was another beautiful day with only one ingredient missing—his wife.

He considered making a pot of coffee but the feeling he'd had last night, a sort of vague fear of being alone, deterred him. Instead, he splashed cold water on his face and combed his hair and put on a clean shirt. Then he walked down the road to the clubhouse.

The younger set in the community woke up early. Several teenagers and pre-teens were splashing in the pool. Brunnhilde was sitting on the diving board rubbing suntan oil on her legs.

"Hi," she greeted him. "Hey. What happened to your face after Herman and I saw you at The Golden Bull?"

Fingering the still tender knuckle cuts and the contusions on his face, he said, "I had a minor accident. Is there anything new on Sally?"

Brunnhilde shook her head. "Not as far as I know. But have you heard the really big news? Have you heard about Tasy and Andy?"

Harris stood with one foot on the anchored end of the diving board. "What about them?"

"They're getting married late this afternoon. Then they're going to drive to Mexico City and catch a plane for Buenos Aires. And after a two-week honeymoon, Andy's father is going to make him assistant manager of his travel bureau."

"In Buenos Aires?"

"Uh-huh."

Harris considered the information. "When did all this happen?"

"Last night. After Tasy rode home from Acapulco with you. Anyway, that's when they decided to get married." Brunnhilde applied suntan lotion to her inner thighs. "Not that I was too surprised. Like we told you at Papa Juarez's, Andy and Tasy were going steady long before he and Sally started fooling around."

"Yes. So you did," Harris said. "What does Tasy's mother think about her getting married?"

Brunnhilde returned the stopper to the bottle of lotion, felt to make sure the crotch strap of her bikini was giving her a reasonable amount of coverage and stretched out full length on the board with her head resting on her interlaced fingers. "Who knows? She's still in Mexico City, honeying around some spick producer, trying, to get him to give her a part in a picture. But she wouldn't care if she did know. She doesn't care what Tasy does."

"Who told you that?"

"Tasy."

Harris went on around the pool to the open door of the combination bar and dining room. That explained the earnest conversation he'd witnessed between Tasy and Carlson senior last night. He gave Tasy a capital A for effort. The teenager with the auburn hair not only knew what she wanted, she'd gotten it. She'd gotten Andy Carlson. And he could imagine her line of reasoning when she talked to Andy's father. She'd probably pointed out that even if Andy had been playing house with Sally Ti and had gotten the Eurasian girl pregnant, when General Ti did locate his daughter he couldn't very well insist that young Carlson marry her if he was honeymooning in Buenos Aires.

The wives of Pepe or Juan had not shown up for duty as yet but Señor Córdoba, wearing a freshly laundered white mess jacket, was alternating between serving breakfast to Colonel and Mrs. Amapa and Mr. and Mrs. Gottlieb and pouring the foundation for Jack Wilder's daily state of intoxication.

Harris went through the usual *buenos días* routine

with Córdoba, then sat at the bar and ordered a cup of coffee and some scrambled eggs and toast.

Córdoba phrased it delicately, "Then you are still a *soltero* this morning, *Señor?* Your so gracious *Señora* remained in Acapulco overnight?"

"So it seems," Harris said. "How about the general? Did he ever phone Mrs. Ti?"

"No, *Señor,*" Córdoba said. "He did not. Nor have I seen him this morning." He sighed. "It could be I am wrong but I am still of the opinion he should have called the *policia.*"

Jack Wilder emptied the shot glass in front of him and pushed it across the bar for a refill. "I assume you gentlemen are talking about that charade in the lounge yesterday morning?"

"*Si,*" Córdoba said.

The one-time psychiatrist said thoughtfully, "I've been thinking about that. And do you know what I think?"

"What?" Harris asked.

"That's just what it was, a charade. I used to have quite a number of cases like that. I mean where some dewy-eyed girl from a strict family finally learned the facts of life and went overboard for some joy pole." He looked at Señor Córdoba. "No offense intended, understand? But running the road to Acapulco every day the way most of these kids do, I think she probably met some good-looking, heavy-hung young Mex and spent the two days she was supposed to be spending with a girl friend with him. Then when she decided to come home, he followed her. Then after they tore off a few more of the same, after she sneaked out of the house to meet him, they staged the scene in the lounge to throw her father off the trail. And then she lit out with him again. Either that or she's been beating the mattress with one of the boys or maybe one of the married men living here. And he knocked her higher than the proverbial kite and she's taken off to have something done about it."

Córdoba mopped at a wet place on the bar. "General Ti mentioned that possibility yesterday morning. That was why he was reluctant to report her disappearance. He said, if she had been guilty of an indiscretion he would prefer to keep the matter in the family. But he also said if it transpired that she'd been harmed, he could take care of that, too."

Wilder was amused. "Well, don't look at me." He sipped his drink and added, "As the old saying goes, you never miss the violets until old age sticks a calla lily in your fly. A funny thing, life. When a man is young and perpetually randy he never stops to think there may be a day when he's afraid some girl will say 'Yes' and embarrass hell out of him."

Marcia Wilder and Sonia were friends but Harris didn't know too much about Wilder. As with most of the men living in the enclave, what he did know was rumor and hearsay. But he'd heard it said that Wilder, at one time prominent in psychiatric circles, had lost his license because he had overtaxed his rusty medical skills in performing an abortion on one of his younger and prettier patients whom he'd gotten into trouble under the guise of releasing her inhibitions.

"I'm bleeding for you," Harris said.

In lieu of oil on troubled waters, Señor Córdoba poured more hot coffee in Harris' cup.

"You both have heard, of course, that Señorita Lane and Andy Carlson are to be married this afternoon?"

Harris finished his eggs. "Yes. So Brunnhilde just informed me."

"You're lucky," Wilder said. "I don't know where

Marcia gets her information but she couldn't wait to tell me. I got a blow by blow description of the proposed nuptials before I could pry my eyes open." Sitting as he was, with his elbows resting on the bar, the doctor had a box-seat view of the diving board through the open door. He sucked in his breath, then exhaled slowly. "Well, what do you know? I'll be damned. That's one Krafft-Ebing missed. Maybe if I wrote a paper on it the A.M.A. would take me back in the club."

"*Perdone?*" Córdoba said, puzzled.

Wilder grinned. "Maybe I'm not as old as I thought I was. Either that or I have a mole fetish. That kid out on the diving board just tugged the strap of her bikini aside to scratch herself and she has a mole in the goddamndest place."

Señor Córdoba glanced hastily at Mrs. Amapa and Mrs. Gottlieb to make certain they hadn't overheard.

"*Por favor, Señor.* There are women present."

Harris drank the last of his coffee and stood up. Wilder disgusted him. He signed his tab and walked off without saying goodby.

He'd almost reached the door when the phone on the end of the bar rang and Córdoba picked up the receiver. "Rancho Paraíso clubhouse and bar. Señor Corboda speaking." He listened for a moment and said, "*Si.* It so happens he is here now," then inclined his head at Harris. "It is for you, *Señor.*"

"Sonia?" Harris asked hopefully.

"No," Córdoba said. "It is a Señorita Fillmore. And she says it is *muy* important that she speak with you right away."

"Jim here, Elsie," Harris said into the phone. "Has Sonia gotten in touch with you?"

"No. Not exactly," the agent said. "But I know where she is. It seems she took an overdose of sleeping pills in a room at the Hotel Los Amigos."

"Good God!"

"They think she's going to be all right, Jim. But you'd better drive in right away. Come to my office first and we'll go to her together."

"I'm on my way," Harris said.

Before he could cradle the phone, Elsie added, "And while I don't see how the two incidents can have any connection, there's something else I think you should know. Carlos just came back from the Federal Building and one of his fellow officers told him the local police found Abdul Ahmed dead on the floor of his studio this morning."

"Dead from what?"

"Two bullet holes in his head. And there was some tangible evidence that he'd been sexually intimate with a woman shortly before he was killed."

Harris digested this information and repeated, "I'm on my way."

He cradled the phone and left the bar and found that Brunnhilde was no longer alone on the diving board. Tasy had joined her but not a Tasy he'd ever seen before.

Probably in preparation for her hastily planned marriage to Andy Carlson, she'd piled her long auburn hair on top of her head in a becoming bouffant hairdo. A pair of expensive diamond earrings, undoubtedly her mother's, dangled from her ears. Artfully applied makeup covered most of her freckles. Instead of a playsuit or bikini, she wore a white silk halter that complimented her small but exquisite breasts, and a pair of smart ankle-length white silk slacks. The child looked five years older this morning but her eyes were no longer troubled. As she sat on one edge of the board swinging her sandaled feet and crimson toenails, her smile mirrored her happiness.

"Hi," she said when she saw him. "Thanks again for driving me home last night, Mr. Harris."

"My pleasure," Harris said automatically as he skirted the diving board and started up the hill for his car. "Brunnhilde tells me you and Andy are being married this afternoon."

"That's right," Tasy called after him. "And I expect we'll be very happy."

Chapter Sixteen

For a moment Harris thought the black Cadillac parked in front of the arcade in which Elsie had her office was General Ti's. Then he saw it was an official car chauffeured by a Yaqui Indian wearing the uniform and stripes of a sergeant in the Rurales.

Elsie and Colonel Romez were waiting for him in the back seat of the car. "You and Carlos have met," Elsie said as Harris opened the door and got into the back seat with them.

"Of course." Colonel Romez smiled as he offered Harris his hand. "We had drinks together at the Villa Vera Racquet Club one night."

Harris shook the offered hand, then asked Elsie, "I don't suppose you have heard anything more about Sonia?"

"No," Elsie said. "I'd just opened the office when Mrs. Meier phoned. And she didn't go into detail."

"Who is she?" Harris asked.

"The wife of the resident manager of the Hotel Los Amigos."

"What did she say?"

"Well, she began by asking if I knew a Mrs. James

Harris, and described Sonia. I told her I was not only her agent, but also a good friend, so she told me what she'd called to say. You're sure you want to hear this, Jim?"

"I have to hear it sooner or later."

"She said a number of hotel employees had seen Sonia enter the hotel shortly after midnight last night with one of their guests, a Lieutenant Commander Paul Edwards, neither of them feeling any pain."

"In other words, they were stinking."

"In other words. Then this morning when the maid on the floor entered Edwards' suite to clean it she found Sonia asleep or unconscious in the bedroom. Something about the way she was lying, and her color, caused the maid to believe she was ill. She called the desk and the desk clerk called the house doctor."

"Who discovered she'd tried to kill herself."

"That's right."

"Then later Mrs. Meier went through Sonia's wallet and found a card requesting that in case of an accident either you or I be informed."

"And, under the circumstances, Mrs. Meier thought she'd better call you."

"Yes."

"How many sleeping pills did she take?"

"Mrs. Meier didn't know when she talked to me. She did say the doctor thought he had been called in time. And while Sonia may have a few rough hours, she'll be all right."

"And that bit about Abdul Ahmed?"

Romez said, "If I may speak, Señor Harris, I doubt very much if his demise has anything at all to do with your *Señora*. The local officers to whom I spoke said that his death occurred early yesterday evening and from a few discreet inquiries I instigated, I was able to ascertain that Señora Harris had been in Lieutenant Commander Edwards' company for some time. In fact one of my informants told me they were seen drinking at the Hilton bar as early as two o'clock yesterday afternoon."

"You guys don't miss much, do you?" Harris said.

"Not much," Colonel Romez admitted.

"Then I suppose they know I was there last night."

"No," the Rurale officer admitted. "But Elsie mentioned that fact to me when I arrived at her apartment shortly after you left last night." He added, "In the course of general conversation when I inquired after the health of your *Señora.*"

"And you didn't tell the local boys?"

"No."

"Why not?"

Colonel Romez said dryly, "Because from what my friend on the local force tells me, according to the post mortem, among his other findings the police surgeon noted that the deceased had been intimate with a member of the opposite sex shortly before his demise."

"There was a girl there when I was."

"Did you see her?"

"No."

Romez lost interest in the subject. "From what little I know of the deceased's character, and from what Elsie has told me, the young woman, whoever she was, undoubtedly had good reason to do what she did." He spoke softly into the speaking tube. The Indian driver turned on the siren, then clomped one booted foot down on the accelerator. The big car hurtled through heavy mid-morning traffic, scattering pedestrians like chickens and causing the cursing drivers of other cars to swerve out of its way or brake to squeaking stops.

In his youth Max Meier, the resident manager of the Hotel Los Amigos, had owned and been the leader of one of pre-World War II Germany's most popular dance bands.

He was blond. He had blue eyes. He could trace an unblemished Germanic genealogy back to Frederick the Great. He was a talented musician. Wherever he and his band played they attracted capacity crowds. Unfortunately, for that particular period in history, he had two serious flaws in his character. While he himself was of pure Aryan stock, Max had, unpatriotically, permitted himself to fall in love with and marry the vivacious raven-haired girl who sang with his band and whose mother, by her own admission had been Jewish.

His second flaw, possibly induced by the times, had been an unquenchable sense of humor. The end had come one night when he had played a command performance at which the newly constituted *Fuehrer* had been the guest of honor.

During the performance, Meier had committed unpardonable sins. He had substituted a swing version of "The Watch on the Rhine" for the scheduled "Horst Wessel" song. Even worse, when the time for his specialty came, he had walked down on the apron of the stage and done an excruciatingly funny, if very pornographic, telephone monologue concerning the predicament of an amorous concentration-camp commander faced with a very serious problem who was phoning Herr Himmler asking for advice.

Meier had barely gotten out of the theatre, and out of Germany, in time.

Now, almost thirty years later, eighteen of them spent in Acapulco, still married to the same wife, with five grown children and a dozen grandchildren who spoke better Spanish than German, Meier frequently spoke of returning to *der Vaterland—mañana.*

Meier was waiting under the ornate canopy of the Hotel Los Amigos when the official black Cadillac glided to a stop in front of the hotel.

"Señorita Fillmore," Colonel Romez introduced them. "And Señor Harris, the young lady's husband."

The hotel man acknowledged the introductions with a wary nod, then looked back at the colonel of Rurales. "Come on, Carlos. Have a heart. The local boys promised me they would keep this as quiet as they could. Where does the federal government come in on a would-be suicide?"

"We don't," Romez assured him. "It merely so happens that Señorita Fillmore and myself were discussing other matters when Hannah so graciously phoned her and I am here in a strictly unofficial capacity." He added, "Also to discourage any unfavorable publicity that might result to one of Señorita Fillmore's clients."

"That's a relief," Meier said.

"How is my wife?" Harris asked him.

"We think out of danger by now," Meier said as he led the way across the lobby to the elevators.

"Is the man still upstairs?"

Meier shook his head. "No. Last night was the last night of the commander's leave. He was flying to San Diego this morning to rejoin his ship."

Harris tried to think of something to say. He couldn't. What did a husband say under the circumstances?

The suite was on the twelfth floor, with a good view of the bay and the wooded mountains on the far side.

As the hotel man opened the door, a slim woman with prematurely gray hair got up from the chair in which she was sitting and held out her hand to Romez.

"It's nice to see you, Carlos."

Romez pressed her hand to the breast of his short uniform jacket as he bowed from the hips. "The pleasure is always mine, Hannah. Every time we meet you have grown more beautiful."

"Hah," Mrs. Meier scoffed. "I'll bet you tell that to all the old hags you know. But don't stop on my account. I love it." She nodded pleasantly to Elsie, then to Harris. "I know you're worried. Doctor Morales assures me that Mrs. Harris is completely out of danger. That is if we can keep her awake until the stimulant counteracts the stuff she took."

While she was speaking the hotel doctor came out of the bedroom.

"The young lady is doing fine," he said "Her pulse is almost normal, most of the cyanosis has disappeared. She is still slightly nauseated from having her stomach pumped up but, in another eight or ten hours she should be fine."

He cased his stethoscope. "But if I were you, Hannah, I'd keep her walking for another ten or fifteen minutes. And if you can, try to get her to talk. Help her get rid of whatever is troubling her."

"Can't I help?" Elsie asked. "Can't I walk her?"

"I presume," Doctor Morales said, "you are the friend Mrs. Meier phoned?"

"Yes."

"Good friends?"

"Yes."

Dr. Morales fastened the hasps on his bag. "In that case I think Hannah had better continue to do the honors." He explained. "You see, as in most of these cases, the young lady is not only very angry with me for having saved her life, she is also very depressed. She will be much more apt to confide in a stranger than in a friend."

"Whatever you say," Elsie said.

Hannah Meier picked her package of cigarettes and her lighter from the end table. "I'll do what I can. But before I go in there again, may I ask you a question, Mr. Harris?"

"Of course."

"You know, at least it is obvious, that your wife came here with a man."

"As you say," Harris said, "that is obvious."

"And knowing that, you still love her and want her back?"

"Yes."

"Good. That gives me something to build on. Now one more question. Your wife's accent intrigues me. Where is Mrs. Harris from originally?"

"Austria. She was born and raised in Vienna."

"Of course. I should have known. She and I are practically *Landsmann.*"

Sonia wished people would leave her alone. What she did with her life was her business. If the maid hadn't come in at the wrong time she wouldn't ever have had to worry about anything again. But right now all she wanted to do was sleep. She tried to snuggle her head into the pillow and felt hands tugging at her again. A voice speaking in fluent German said:

"Oh, no we don't. The doctor said we should walk. From one end of the Ringstrasse to the other if we have to. Up on your feet, *Fraulein.*"

Groaning, Sonia allowed the hands to pull her to

her feet and guide her, half walking, half stumbling, from the big double bed to the closed door of the room, then back again.

"Who are you?" she asked wanly.

Continuing to speak in German, Hannah said, "You don't know me. But I was in before. My name is Hannah Meier and my husband manages the hotel. I was born in Garmisch-Partenkirchen."

Even wanting to go back to sleep as desperately as she did, Sonia was mildly intrigued. "I know where that is. It's halfway between Oberammergau and the Austrian border."

"That's right."

"Now may I go back to sleep?"

"No," Hannah said. "For one reason you're too young and pretty to slip away from us now. For another, boards of directors are funny. And I wouldn't want my husband to get fired just because some mixed-up broad decides she's tired of living. It gives the hotel a bad name."

"I'm not a broad," Sonia said angrily. "I'm a respectable married woman."

"I'm glad to hear it, my dear. So few respectable married women are found in strange men's beds. Especially when they are wearing as little as you were when I first saw you this morning."

"How dare you—" Sonia began. Then she begged, "Please. Go away and let me die. I'm so ashamed."

That's better, Hannah thought. She studied Sonia's face. "If I let you sit in a chair for a few minutes, will you promise not to go to sleep again? Promise to keep on talking?"

"I'll try."

Hannah lit two cigarettes and put one of them between Sonia's lips. "Puff. Puff hard. It may help clear away some of those cobwebs."

Sonia tried to do as she was told. "Why should you care?"

Hannah drew up another chair and sat facing her. "To start with we have one basic problem in common. We're both women. And while I don't know what this is all about, I've been over a few hurdles. Besides, when you reach my age, you can't help having learned some of the facts of life. Not when you start out as a stupid little girl born in a place with the impossible name of Garmisch-Partenkirchen and end up the featured singer of a swing band."

Sonia was mildly interested. "Where did you sing with the band?"

"In Berlin. And most of the other capitals of Europe."

"When?"

"That was a long time ago," Hannah said. "Two or three years before you were born."

Chapter Seventeen

"I was good at it, too," Hannah said. "They called me the young Marlene Dietrich. Only I think I was better. I had more of what counted, and all of it in the right places. You should have heard the men whistle at *me*."

Sonia tried to take her cigarette from her mouth. The paper stuck to her lower lip.

"Men," she said drowsily.

Hannah retrieved the cigarette and snuffed it. She forced Sonia to her feet and into motion again.

"Look, Sonia, I don't know what your problem is. I don't particularly care. I'm merely trying to point out that nothing has ever happened to you that I haven't been through. Now when I phoned that number I found in your purse, a Miss Fillmore answered. She—"

"Then Elsie knows?"

"Both she and your husband do."

"Oh, no. You didn't call Jim?"

"No, I didn't. But she must have. Anyway, they are both out in the other room now. And for whatever consolation it may be your husband still loves and wants you. So, one woman to another, why don't you tell me why you did what you tried to do? You are a model?"

"Yes." Sonia brushed her hair back from her forehead with one hand. "There are pictures of me hanging all over Acapulco. Not very nice pictures, I'm afraid. But—"

"Then this problem of yours is connected with your profession?"

"In a way."

"Well, I don't know anything about modeling. But as I've said, I was a singer with a band. And I'll match those dirty-minded musicians and talent agents and stage-door Johnnies against the field."

"May I please sit down again?" Sonia asked meekly.

"Will you keep on talking?"

"I promise," Sonia promised.

The effect of the barbiturate was wearing off. For the moment she didn't even feel sleepy. All she felt was cold and cheap and very ashamed of herself. She snugged the skirt of the heavy robe someone had put on her around her legs. Then, weeping silently as she talked, speaking in her native tongue, in desperate need to confide in someone who might understand, she told Hannah Meier things she hadn't even told Elsie.

"I'm not excusing myself," she said. "When I left the

house yesterday I didn't mean for things to turn out this way. I was merely furious with Jim. Then I met Paul and we began to drink and one thing led to another." She shrugged. "And when he asked me to come up here with him and let him make love to me, I thought why not? At least he wanted me. And that was more than Jim did."

Her voice turned bleak. "When I woke up this morning he was gone. I'd expected that. He'd told me he had to catch an early-morning plane to rejoin his ship. All I felt at first was a sort of emptiness. I was a little sick from liquor, but otherwise—just empty. Then I began to think, and I felt dirty. Very dirty. I made myself get up. I went to the bathroom. I turned on the water in the shower. I even took a long tub bath. But it didn't do any good. Water wouldn't wash away what I'd done."

It was her story. Hannah let her tell it, hoping the emotional outpouring would help.

Sonia made an expressive gesture with her hands. "I remember that after I'd toweled I sat on the edge of the tub and cried for a long time, feeling sorry for myself I suppose, realizing I'd lost Jim forever, knowing I wouldn't ever dare face him again. Then, thinking perhaps a drink might help, I walked out into the living room looking for a bottle. And then I saw the note and the money on one of the end tables. Three thousand *pesos,* the money Paul had won at the jai alai games."

Sonia wept silently for a moment. "*'To buy a pretty'* the note read. He hadn't even bothered to sign his name. As far as Lieutenant Commander Paul Edwards was concerned, I was just another blonde professional he'd laid and paid for."

Sonia walked to the door and back without

Hannah's assistance. "I'd been over that route before. I didn't want to go it again. I didn't intend to. I tore up the bills and flushed them down the toilet. Then I remembered the sleeping pills I'd bought. I found my purse and swallowed a dozen pills and went back to bed. And now everything I have is gone." She sat down again. "I really wish I didn't have to live."

"You have a problem," Hannah admitted. She hesitated, then went on. "So just in case it may help a little, I'm going to tell you something I've never told anyone else."

Hannah lit two cigarettes and gave one of them to Sonia. "You think it was tough to be a pretty teenager in occupied Vienna? You should have been a pretty Jewess, God forbid, in pre-war Germany. Even a pretty half Jewess who had never been in a temple or a synagogue in her life. You see, when my mother and father were married she loved him enough to promise to raise any children they might have as Catholics. And that was the way I was raised. I could say a Hail Mary or make an act of contrition with the best of them, but I didn't know a prayer shawl from a *yarmelke*.

"But that didn't matter in pre-war Germany. Because one set of my grandparents had been Jewish, I was a candidate for a yellow badge. And because I was in the public eye I was also fair game for any S.S. officer or Gestapo rat who took a fancy to me. I was only a Jew wench who didn't dare complain. Believe me, I had to develop some fancy footwork." Hannah shrugged. "I won some. I lost a few."

Hannah smoked in silence for a moment.

"I was married to Max by then, very happily married, and very much in love. One night our band had to entertain the delegates to a big trade fair in

Düsseldorf. By then things had gotten so bad for my people that Max felt that he had to do something. Felt he had to stand up and be counted. After all, it was his Germany, too.

"So, with *der Fuehrer* himself sitting in the audience, Max got things off to a good start by swinging 'The Watch on the Rhine' instead of playing the 'Horst Wessel' song. Then, not content with that, he did a very funny little monologue about a beer-bellied concentration-camp commander who was playing patty cake with one of his charges who happened to be half Jewish." Hannah smiled wryly. "It seems orders came down from the top to liquidate all the Jews in his camp, and the slob couldn't decide which half of his girl friend to send to the gas ovens."

Hannah snuffed her cigarette. "As far as we were concerned, that was *der Tag*. We had to get out—fast. I don't mean out of Düsseldorf. I mean out of the country. We kept to the back roads. We drove all night, trying to make the Dutch border. But when we got there it was closed. S.S. and Gestapo and regular army men were patrolling the barbed wire. There was only one thing we could do. Max doubled back a few miles and had me check into a small town hotel while he went out and beat the countryside for some member of the local underground who might be willing to risk his neck smuggling us through the barbed wire."

Hannah straightened the cigarette she'd snuffed and tried, vainly, to suck it back to life. "It was one of those German country hotels you see on picture postal cards. Complete with a fire place in every room and a big wood box and a fat innkeeper in a white apron and *Lederhosen.*" She returned the cigarette to the ash tray. "Well, anyway, I'd been there about an hour when there was a knock on the door. Thinking it was

Max, I unlocked and opened it. But it wasn't Max. It was Oberleutnant Kleinschmidt, a big blond S.S. man who had been giving me a bad time for months. It seems he had figured out what we would do when we found the border closed and had offered a reward for any information concerning us, and even though I had registered under another name, the innkeeper had recognized me and turned me in.

"The lieutenant offered me a proposition—if I would 'cooperate' with him while Max was out looking for a guide, he would make it his business to see that Max found one. And also, he would report back to S.S. headquarters that we had escaped and there was no point in continuing to search for us."

Hannah's eyes met those of Sonia. Sonia nodded, smiling faintly.

"I could have been lily pure," Hannah said. "I could have pointed to the door and told him what he could do with his dirty proposition—and wound up in Buchenwald or Dachau.

"But no, my dear. At some time in her life almost every woman allows some man with whom she isn't in love to possess her. For money or a better job. Because she is attracted to him physically. To get even with some other man. To protect someone she loves. So I didn't scream for help. It wasn't there anyway. At the time I tried to tell myself I was doing it for Max. But that wasn't the real reason. I was young. I was pretty. I had talent. I was frightened. I didn't want to die. So I did what the lieutenant wanted me to do. I peeled off my clothes and I got into bed and I cooperated.

"Whatever Oberleutnant Kleinschmidt wanted to do to me—*wunderbar*. Whatever he wanted me to do to him— *jawohl*. What was a little flesh between a half Jewish canary and a member of the master race?"

Hannah lighted a fresh cigarette. "It went on like that all day. When he finally left, it was night and I barely had strength enough left to walk the few hundred yards to the grove of linden trees on the edge of town where I was supposed to meet Max. As the lieutenant had promised, he'd found a guide. And two hours later we were in Holland."

Sonia cleared her throat. "And you never told your husband what happened?"

"I've never told anyone until now."

"Then why tell me?"

Hannah studied the younger woman's face. The last of the faint blue tinge was gone. Her pupils were no longer constricted. Her breathing was deep and regular. It should be safe to allow her to sleep.

"I think you can figure that out," Hannah said. "If I've lived with that all these years, you ought to be able to live with yourself. No permanent damage has been done."

"I—see what you mean," Sonia said. Her drowsiness had returned, but it seemed natural this time. It was an effort for her to speak. "But I can't possibly face Jim now."

"You don't have to," Hannah said. She stripped the soiled linen from the bed and began to remake it with clean sheets the maid had left behind. "Right now you are going to get about twelve hours of normal sleep, compliments of the Hotel Los Amigos. And when the time comes for you to face your husband, feeling the way he seems to feel about you, knowing men as I do, I don't imagine it's going to make much difference what you tell him. He'll settle for having you home."

She helped Sonia up from the chair and out of the flannel robe and into the freshly made bed. Sonia squeezed her hand.

"Thank you. Thank you for everything, Mrs. Meier."

Hannah held Sonia's hand until her fingers relaxed and lay limp on the sheet. Then she made the sign of the Cross.

Hannah hoped no recording angels had been standing in the wings when she'd told her story. Still, it could have been that way. Everything she'd told Sonia *was* true, up to the point where she'd said:

"... and I cooperated."

She had undressed. She had gotten into bed. She'd been willing to cooperate. She'd fully intended to. As she'd seen it at the time, she'd had no choice.

But right at the critical moment—well, it seemed that Max had made contact with an underground guide much sooner than he had expected. Max had returned to the hotel to get her. And without bothering to knock on the door Max had walked into the room. He was a quick study, Max. His eyes opened wide, and then he simply leaped toward the fireplace.

Oberleutnant Kleinschmidt didn't have a chance to reach for his pistol. She could still close her eyes and hear the crunch when Max parted his Prussian military cut with the heavy poker. For a moment she'd been afraid Max might use the poker on her own bare body. But if youth had problems, it also had compensations.

The guide had had to wait a few more minutes, that was all.

Hannah adjusted the Venetian blind so the sun wouldn't shine in Sonia's eyes, wondering, as she had often wondered through the years, how the pot-bellied innkeeper had reacted when he had opened the lid of the big wood box beside the fireplace.

She imagined he'd been surprised. He'd also had a lot to explain.

Chapter Eighteen

Upriver the peaks of the mountains were veiled by a purple haze. They looked delightfully cool, but here under the trees it was both hot and humid, 102° as recorded by the thermometer hanging in the shade of the overhang of the white-washed adobe *cantina* on the outskirts of Coyuca de Benitez.

Charlie Lee wished General Ti would make up his mind, jump one way or the other. If the old man didn't act, and soon, he was going to have to take other measures—or scrub the mission.

He felt sweat start on the back of his neck at the thought. The party didn't condone failure. You did what you were sent to do or you didn't report back to Peking. If he failed and went back, he would lose his commission and wind up working on some communal farm, probably shoveling dung under the watchful eyes of a pair of the newly constituted Red Guards.

Lee transferred his attention from the glass of lukewarm beer in front of him to his employer's face. The trouble with Ti, he decided, was that living in Mexico had mellowed and softened him. He'd learned how to live with and like *mañana*. Instead of striking out on reflex as the man was reputed to have done before his defection, Ti vacillated. He had become overcautious.

What did he have to do to goad the old man into action, show him a motion picture of young Carlson copulating with his daughter? If he had thought of it, he could have filmed the episode. In the state of sexual excitement Sally had been in when Conchita finished priming her, the kid wouldn't have known, or cared, if the scene of her defloration had been televised and relayed around the world by Telstar.

Then there was the business of Mr. Harris. That was a bad break he hadn't expected. If General Ti was still the man he was reputed to have been, he'd have killed the artist with his bare fists five seconds after he saw the dirty picture someone had painted of the three girls. And if Ti had killed Harris, by now he would be in custody, awaiting trial or deportation— and Lee could be in an air-conditioned commercial jet bound for Peking to report he'd accomplished his mission.

But no. Instead of reacting as he should have, Ti hadn't laid a hand on the artist. He hadn't even returned to the enclave to confer with Mrs. Ti, giving Lee time to row out to the ketch and relieve Conchita. Instead, the old man had insisted on accompanying Lee and Toy on a dreary repetition of their already extensive search of the places where Sally *might* be.

And here they were at two o'clock the next afternoon, without one damn thing accomplished, sitting in a grimy *cantina* on the outskirts of a stinking copra center, 25 miles northwest of Acapulco, waiting for a "meet" with the agent of the local *sindicato*.

Lee used his handkerchief on the back of his neck. Conchita was probably out of her mind by now wondering what had happened to him. And if the nurse should panic and allow Sally to get away before Ti did something to attract official attention to himself—there went the entire caper.

Ti said, "Is the heat making you uncomfortable, Charlie?"

"A little," Lee admitted. "How long do we wait here?"

"Until Señor Guerrero arrives."

Harry Toy was concerned. "Meanwhile, what about

Sally?"

"This meeting concerns my daughter," the general said. "I have a small proposition to offer Señor Guerrero."

Lee said, "Look, I don't want to cross you, boss, but I think what we ought to do is go back to Rancho Paraíso and talk to young Carlson. If necessary beat the truth out of him. Because all of the kids I talked to yesterday afternoon told me in so many words that since the Carlson punk broke up with the Lane girl, he and Sally have been, well, more than friends."

General Ti remained unruffled. "That's possible. When we find her, Sally will tell us."

It made Lee nervous to watch Ti. He walked to the door of the *cantina* and looked out. From where he was standing the small copra center wasn't much of a town. All he could see were a few scrawny chickens scratching in the dust, half a dozen housewives doing the family wash in the river, and endless rows of palm trees. He'd been told there were seven million of them in the narrow one-hundred-and-fifty-mile-long coastal strip. He believed it. The natives sold the meat of the nuts to be used in soaps and margarines, the husks for fuel and brushes and mats and insulating material, drank the milk to supplement their diet, and used the fronds to roof their houses. Still, when you'd seen one palm tree, you'd seen them all.

Lee looked back at his employer. Could it be that the shock of his daughter's disappearance had turned the old man senile? He'd heard of such things happening. It could be the reason Ti had insisted on both Lee and Toy staying close to him. He was afraid to be alone.

Lee resumed his contemplation of the palm trees. If he couldn't goad Ti into action he had one alternative. All he had to do was phone the Acapulco narcotics squad. Ten minutes later the Federals would be chopping down the doors of Ti's warehouse.

Once inside they would find 25 kilos of pure heroin fresh from Kowloon and Ti would be through. The only trouble with that pat solution was, Ti's known employees would wind up doing 20 years each in some stinking Mexican prison.

Lee considered the shipment. It might be treason, but a man had to look out for himself. Since this new power struggle had begun, he wasn't so sure he wanted to go back to China. For all he knew, his own immediate superiors had been purged.

With the price of uncut heroin sold locally holding steady at 350 dollars an ounce, 16 ounces to the pound and a kilo weighing 2.2046 pounds, that came to roughly 5,600 dollars a kilo. Twenty-five times that was 140,000 dollars. And the same 25 kilos selling wholesale for 140,000 dollars in Mexico, transported to Chicago's Loop or New York's Times Square or San Francisco's Embarcadero, cut with milk-sugar powder and parceled out to the ounce men and the pushers could make a man a multimillionaire.

Ti trusted him. He had a key to the warehouse. The stuff only weighed between 50 and 60 pounds. And if worse came to worse he could pack the stuff into a suitcase, grab a plane to the border and play it by ear from there. And Ti wouldn't dare to report its loss.

Lee transferred his attention to a rapidly moving car. He watched it until it crossed the bridge over the river, then resumed his chair at the table.

"I think Guerrero is coming now."

The car turned off the road and braked in a swirl of dust and squawking of chickens. Guerrero, a compactly built man about the same age as Ti, came into the *cantina* accompanied by two youthful, swaggering *pistoleros*.

"I hear you want to see me, General," he said as he sat at the table.

"Yes," General Ti replied. "I do. On a matter of business. How would your people like to buy 25 kilos of uncut merchandise at bargain-basement prices?"

"The people I represent," Señor Guerrero said, "are always interested in good merchandise. But why the bargain, General Ti? You've always been a hard man to deal with."

"I need a substantial amount of cash in a hurry," Ti said. "It seems I have a slight family problem."

Guerrero glanced at Charlie Lee and Harry Toy. "It was brought to my attention that your boys have been asking around. Something concerning your daughter. But what does that have to do with you needing money?"

General Ti took a folded sheet of his business stationery from his pocket and handed Guerrero the notice he'd had his secretary type before leaving his office. It was written in Spanish and addressed to the editor of the leading Acapulco newspaper. Señor Guerrero translated it into English as he read it aloud:

REWARD

General Luang Ti of Rancho Paraíso will pay $100,000 reward for any information leading to the discovery of the current whereabouts of his sixteen-year-old daughter, Lotus Ti, commonly known as Sally. All information received will be treated as confidential and the communicator's identity protected.

"Now hold it. Hold it just one goddamn minute, boss," Charlie Lee said hotly. "There's no need of you running a thing like that. Harry and I have been doing the best we can."

"Have you found Sally?"

"No," Lee admitted. "Not yet." He tried to save his ace in the hole. "But if you start offering that kind of money for information, the Federal men are going to wonder how you came up with that much lettuce. And the next thing you know they're going to go through the warehouse with a vacuum cleaner."

"True," General Ti admitted. "But if the men whom Señor Guerrero represents buy our merchandise before I send the notice to the paper, there won't be anything for them to find except a few crates of brass Mandarin incense burners, carved ivory back scratchers, and such other trivia."

"I know. But—"

"How about you, Harry?" Ti asked.

"Well," Toy said thoughtfully, "the stuff is worth forty grand more. But you're the boss. All I do is take orders. And I know how I'd feel if Sally was my kid."

Guerrero laid the notice face down on the table. "Frankly your family problems are none of my concern, General Ti. But the men whom I represent are not adverse to an advantageous deal. Do you want to sell or don't you?"

"I want to sell."

"You say you have 25 kilos?"

"That's right."

"Local stuff?"

"No. From Kowloon, via a Dutch freighter."

"How do I know it's pure?"

Ti laid a plastic envelope sealed with adhesive tape on the table. "Have your chemist test it. If you like what he finds, I'll meet you in my office tonight at eight o'clock. You bring the money. I'll have the merchandise."

Señor Guerrero put the envelope in his coat pocket. "If the merchandise turns out what you represent it to be, you have a deal."

General Ti said, quietly, "And, by the way, you can tell your people this will be the last shipment I'll handle. From now on, I intend to live off of my legitimate business."

Señor Guerrero considered the information and smiled, thinly. "I doubt that, General. Oh, I know how you feel. Right now, with your daughter missing, you're wondering if it may not be some form of retribution. But anyone who uses the stuff is going to get it somewhere. And they might as well buy it from us." He nodded to his *pistoleros* to precede him, then turned in the doorway of the *cantina*. "And while, as I said before, it isn't any of my concern, I, too, have a teenage daughter. So—*buena suerte*. I hope you find your daughter unharmed."

"Thank you," General Ti said gravely as he tested the blade of the knife on his thumb. "No matter what a man may endeavor to do, it is always nice to have luck on his side."

Chapter Nineteen

Feminine reactions to the impending nuptials were varied. While they despised Cara Lane, most of the women liked Tasy and were genuinely happy for her. They felt she was making a good marriage. There were a few, however, who insisted over the bridge tables that had been set up on the flagging rimming the pool that neither she nor Andy was mature enough for marriage and it probably wouldn't last more than two or three months at the most.

Then there were those who had put together two and two and what had been discovered in the lounge the morning before and argued rather warmly that Andy had probably gotten Sally Ti pregnant and Andy's father was merely making the best of a bad situation by getting his son safely married and out of the country before the Chinese girl returned and she and her father attempted to cut in on the Carlson money by filing a paternity suit.

"Not," Mrs. Schilling said smugly, "that a suit would have much standing in a country where the technical definition of a virgin is a girl who is able to outrun her father and brothers. These people here don't have any morals at all. I hear that out in the back country the Indian girls start having relations when they are nine or ten years old and when their oldest child is five or six years old they push him out of their *jacal,* or whatever those funny-looking houses they live in are called, to make room for their most recent bastard."

"That's what I've heard," Mrs. Mitchell said. "Of course, I don't imagine the upper classes are much different from us. But John says the Indians and the peons breed like animals. Wherever they happen to be, whenever the mood strikes them."

Blushing at the delicacy of the subject being discussed, but wanting desperately to be one of the group, young Mrs. Amapa pointed out, "But the Ti girl isn't a native. And while as in my native country, Chinese girls frequently marry at an early age, her family would lose much face if she were to become *enceinte* before she and her intended sought out the blessings of a priest."

Mrs. Gottlieb shrugged. "That's true. But she didn't take off all her clothes to go swimming in the pool. You know, I'm beginning to think it doesn't much matter what country you're in or what a girl's background may be, it seems to be about all any of the little sluts ever think about."

"Oh, I don't know," Mrs. Schilling said defensively. "The boys are just as bad. And I think Karl and I can trust Brunnhilde. We told her all about the birds and bees as soon as she was old enough to understand."

Mrs. Gottlieb studied the dummy, then led a five of spades to get back to the king on the board. "That's good. I mean the birds and bees bit. And I hope you also told her about the flowers. Because while I don't want to be catty or start an argument, from the amount of time that blonde vixen of yours and my Herman spend together, and the damnedest reasons they find to run the roads, I think it's entirely possible that one of these nights she may get some pollen on her." She indicated the wedding preparations going on in the clubhouse lounge. "And if that happens, you and I are going to be going through *that,* my dear."

It was a windfall he hadn't expected. Córdoba couldn't have been more pleased. Mr. Carlson had given him carte blanche. It was to be his best champagne and *langosta* for everyone, plus a cold buffet of sliced ham and freshly delivered *almejas coloradas* and *albondija* and *cueritos* and cheese from Chihuahua. With everyone in the enclave invited.

Córdoba inspected the buffet for the fifth time, then squirted some lime on one of the double-breasted salmon-pink mollusks waiting in their silver-dollar-sized shells and sampled it.

It still wriggled a little as it went down, but it was

deliciosa. Young Señor Carlson and Señorita Lane would have a wedding reception they would remember for all of their lives.

The portly entrepreneur sighed. There were only two sad notes. Unless she returned from Mexico City *pronto,* the bride's mother was going to miss the wedding. The other sad note was Señora Ti, who had resumed her vigil by the phone. Córdoba hoped General Ti called soon. He knew how he would feel if it was one of his daughters who was missing. Especially if he had found her pants and panties and halter beside a couch.

Against that, none of his daughters would have been wearing pants. Panties under their dresses, *si.* But not on the outside. Nor would she have been in an unlighted lounge with a man at two o'clock in the morning unless she was married to him. But then not all fathers were as strict as those of his own people. There were times, and this was one of them, when he was glad he wasn't a nonnational. So few people from other countries, male or female, had any conception of morals.

He turned to help Paquita find a place on the crowded buffet table to set a huge platter of fruits, and was subjected to another tantalizing view of her shapely upper body. He went immediately in search of Pepe and found him opening a large crate of live lobsters packed in wet moss.

"Si," the younger man said earnestly. "I told Paquita just what you told me to tell her when we walked home along the beach last night. But she said no one *had* to look and if *Dios* had not meant her to have breasts, he would have made her a man."

In Dr. Wilder's opinion, two of the most barbaric

customs still extant were marriages and funerals. In the latter a man's grieving widow and relatives and co-workers sang sad paeans about a beautiful isle of somewhere and the dead Joe's chances of reaching a city foursquare. This with him strapped into a coffin, dead before his time of angina pectoris or a perforated ulcer, the only place he was going six feet underground and, if she happened to be young, his grieving widow already eyeing some young stud and wondering how much consolation she could buy with the insurance money.

The other custom was weddings. Stripped to fundamentals, most marriage ceremonies were merely another form of advertising. "Look, maw. I'm going to get laid tonight." This when the chances were the groom had been at the well so many times he'd finally dropped a bucket and that was the real reason for the ceremony.

Wilder sipped at his frozen daiquiri as he watched the preparations for the wedding from a table in the bar.

It was difficult to tell about this one. Considering the haste with which it had been conceived and was being executed it looked to him as if young Carlson had drunk from a Chinese well once too often and his father was making certain that his nineteen-year-old offspring wouldn't be vulnerable to a proposal that he love, cherish, and support either the well or the result of any residue he might have left in its receptive confines.

Five years after he'd lost his license to practice in the only field he knew, Wilder was still bitter. He hadn't seduced Regina Van Pelt with any rubbish anent releasing her inhibitions. She didn't have inhibitions. She had seduced him. And as for the abortion, well, hell, he shouldn't have attempted it, but it certainly hadn't been her first. If he hadn't tried to steady himself with booze, it wouldn't have been her last, either.

Wilder finished his drink. Beautiful, cultured young woman. Regina. Social Register. With no more scruples than a tramp who kissed for her bread. She'd been a delightful bed partner. At his age, he'd been flattered. But because he hadn't performed a curettage for years, and the booze had betrayed him ... well here he was in Mexico.

Wilder looked through the mullioned windows of the bar and saw Andy Carlson standing there, waiting for his bride to arrive. He could take young Carlson or leave him alone. The girl he was marrying, though, was something else.

Wilder looked for Tasy but couldn't see her. He was a little saddened by the thought that, after she was married to young Carlson, he would probably never see her again. The Lane girl had intrigued him ever since she and her mother first moved into the enclave. Most of the teenagers living at Rancho Paraíso were as transparent as a pane of window glass. The Lane girl was different. She had a mind like a steel trap. Wilder mentally rejected the cliché. Portcullis would be a better simile. You could be talking to her and, if you broached some subject she didn't want to discuss or of which she disapproved, you could almost hear the turn of the screw and the clank of the chain as she lowered a protective grating over her gray-green eyes. In the days when he had been practicing, it would have been interesting to have had her on his couch, to learn what really went on behind that intriguing bridge of rapidly fading freckles.

Noting that Paquita had returned to the bar, he

held up his empty glass.

"Por favor."

"Si, Señor." The girl smiled as she took the glass, then practiced her halting English as she wiped vigorously at a small pool of spilled liquid on the table. "How you say, one ver' *frío* daiquiri."

Well, at least I can still look. Wilder thought. *But if I ever go blind, I'm dead.*

Brunnhilde's right garter felt too tight. She loosened it, then readjusted her garter belt before brushing her skirt back into place and resuming putting the final touches on her makeup. She decided she needed a trifle more eye shadow and reached for the tube, then looked over her shoulder as a male voice admired:

"Nice. Very nice, honey. You know, this is the first time I've ever seen you in stockings and high heels."

Brunnhilde turned back to her mirror. "You would show up right then. But don't get any funny ideas. This is a very solemn occasion."

Herman came into the room and sat on the edge of the bed. "Who's getting any funny ideas? You about ready to pick up Tasy?"

"Just about. But it's going to be funny around here without her."

"It will at that."

Brunnhilde smoothed the eye shadow she'd applied. "Herman."

"Yeah?"

"Tell me something, will you?"

"What?"

"Did you ever with her?"

"Don't tell me you're jealous?"

"Could be."

Herman smelled the gardenia on the lapel of his

white dinner jacket. "Well, I could say yes. But if I did I'd be lying. I almost did once, though."

"When was that?"

"You remember the big beach party we had up at the cove to celebrate Cinco de Mayo the first week she and her mother moved into Rancho Paraíso?"

"Yes."

"Well, all the rest of the kids were whooping it up around the fire and Tasy looked kind of lonesome sitting by herself. So I thought I'd give her a break. I walked her up the beach a ways. And after we'd talked for a while I tried to kiss her. She let me, but when I tried to follow it up, it was no dice. She said she had just moved in and from what she'd seen she liked all of us very much and wanted to be one of the crowd. But before she committed herself she wanted to know what the ground rules were."

"That sounds like Tasy. What did you tell her?"

"The truth. That a few of the girls like Sally would let a boy kiss them, but that was as far as they'd go. But the really popular girls, and the ones who had the most dates, were the ones who, if they liked a boy, would let him put his hand on her and put her hand on him."

"What did she say?"

"She said it was about the same as it had been with the crowd she'd run with in Malibu. Then after I'd deep-kissed her a couple of times—she wasn't very enthusiastic about it, more resigned like—she said she supposed we might as well get it over and get back to the gang."

"And did you?"

"No. There was sand or something in the zipper of her trunks and by the time we finally got it unstuck we heard a lot of yelling around the fire and I looked up and saw that Andy had just arrived. And Tasy saw him about the same time and lost all interest in me. Oh, she was very nice about it, like she is about most everything. She said she was sorry if she'd gotten me excited and maybe some other time. Then she zipped up her trunks and asked would I please walk her back to the fire."

"Where you introduced her to Andy and she let him go all the way."

"No," Herman said, thoughtfully. "I don't think so. I was talking to Andy the other day and he said in the two years they'd gone together he and Tasy never had."

Brunnhilde finished smoothing her eye shadow. "That's what Tasy always told me and Sally, but I only half-believed it up until now. No wonder the kid took it so hard when Andy started playing house with Sally." She wiped her fingertips with a piece of tissue and turned around on the bench. "What do you think has happened to Sally, Herman?"

"It beats me."

"Do you really think Andy got her pregnant?"

Herman got up from the bed. "Could be. And if he did that's probably the reason why Mr. Carlson is in such a sweat to get him married to Tasy."

"Probably," Brunnhilde agreed. The long skirt of her formal gown swishing around her ankles, slightly unsteady on the high heels she wasn't accustomed to wearing, she got up from the bench and touched her escort's cheek with her fingers.

"Honey."

"Yeah."

"What would you do if you got me pregnant?"

"Are you?"

"No."

"Then don't scare a guy like that."

"Just suppose."

Herman considered the matter. "Well, the first thing I'd do would be to drive into Acapulco and buy a hat."

"What would you want with a hat?"

"What do you think? To hold in my hand when I went to your father and said, 'Pardon me, Mr. Schilling. As you know, my name is Herman Gottlieb. As you may or may not know, I have been in love with your daughter for some time. Now it seems that someone sold her a bad batch of B.C. pills. So I respectfully ask your permission for her to make an honest man of me.'"

Brunnhilde laughed, but she was pleased. "You mean that, don't you, Herman?"

"Yes."

"Even if I am, well, sort of pudgy?"

"I hear pudgy girls make the best kind of wives. Even if the one I picked does have a mole in the damnedest place."

Brunnhilde rested her face on his shirt front. "What are you trying to do, make me bawl or take off my dress?"

Herman glanced at his watch. "We haven't time. That would mean you would have to make up again. And we should be picking up Tasy right now."

Brunnhilde snuggled closer. "I like you."

"I like you," Herman said. "But let's not get sloppy about it. Not with a bed so handy."

He gripped her elbow and guided her gently but firmly to the bedroom door.

Chapter Twenty

The dreams had never seemed too important. They were merely something that had happened to her over which she'd had no control. Some of them had been pleasant. Others had been embarrassing. There were some she wished she could forget. Still, Tasy hoped, they were merely a passing phase.

When she finished showering and toweling, she powdered her body carefully, then applied a dab of perfume to the lobes of her ears and the fold of flesh under her breasts. She hoped that Andy liked her. Not that he hadn't seen most of her at one time or another, but never all of her at once. That much of what she'd told Mr. Harris was true.

"We can wait for that, honey," Andy had said.

The fly that had invaded the bathroom while she was showering persisted in buzzing around her face. Tasy brushed it away as she studied her reflection in the full-length mirror. She could wish she had more hair. Both Sally and Brunnhilde had twice as much as she did. During the first year she'd gone steady with Andy, because she'd wanted him to be pleased with her, she'd even bought a bottle of hair tonic and had used it religiously, but without any appreciable effect. As she put on the new briefs and the bra Catalina had laid out for her, she consoled herself with the knowledge that her mother had been slighted in the same respect and it didn't seem to make her any less attractive to men. Her mother had been married six times.

Tasy sat on the edge of the tub and shaped a pair of sheer hose to her legs. Not that she ever intended to marry again. She hoped to make Andy a good wife. She meant to be a good wife. She couldn't possibly be more grateful than she was for what Mr. Carlson was doing for them.

This was all like a dream come true.

Tasy slipped into her shoes, then walked into the bedroom to comb her hair and apply her makeup. She wished she hadn't thought of that particular simile.

Not that her dreams were anything recent. As far as she could remember, she'd had her first bad dream when she was six years old. That had been in Istanbul a few months after her mother had married a Shah or a Pasha or something and her British-born American nanny had taken her to visit them.

At the time she had been too young to comprehend fully how beautiful the palace they'd lived in must have been. When she grew older, she'd often wished she could see it again. It had probably been like something straight out of the *Arabian Nights* as illustrated in the unexpurgated copy one of the girls in the school in Switzerland had smuggled in.

As she remembered, there had been a lot of high arches and long halls and she and her nanny had been given a room about the size of the main concourse at Kennedy International.

As she first brushed, then did up her hair, Tasy reflected that first dream had been so long ago that most of the details had faded. But she still remembered certain parts of it distinctly.

In her dream she had awakened in the middle of the night wanting to tinkle, but she didn't remember where the bathroom was. Her nanny had drunk so much wine with her dinner that Tasy hadn't been able to awaken her. So she'd gone in search of her mother. She remembered walking down a seemingly endless series of high vaulted corridors, her bare feet pitter-patting on the tile, opening all of the doors she passed and peering in, hoping they concealed a w.c.

Then, in her dream, she'd found her mother. She'd heard her mother's voice first, panting and sort of moaning as if she was in pain. Then when she opened the door and walked into the room she saw her mother lying on a big couch with cushions all around it and someone had taken off all her clothes and the Shah or the Pasha, or whatever he was kept beating at her with his body and poking a big long white something into her. And every time he hurt her, her mother cried out again.

One corner of Tasy's mouth tugged down. How naive could you be? But then, of course, she'd only been six years old and six-year-old girls weren't supposed to know about such things.

She remembered, frightened as she had been, running across the room and pounding on the man's back and shouting, "You stop hurting my mommy."

Then everything had become confused. She remembered that the man had slapped her so hard she'd tinkled on the floor. Then her mother had been holding her in her arms and shouting back at the man shouting at them. And when she'd awakened the next morning she found her mother sitting on the bed. And after mother kissed her good morning she'd said that as soon as Nanny dressed her they were going to Spain, where she had a contract to make a picture. And when Tasy asked about what had happened the night before her mother had said:

"It was just a bad dream, honey. Forget it."

The fly had followed her into the bedroom and was buzzing around the mirror. Tasy waved it away from her face as she studied her hair. She hoped Andy would like it done up. She thought Mr. Carlson would. It was one of the things he had impressed on her after they'd had their talk and she had pointed out that if she and Andy were married, General Ti couldn't very well force him to marry Sally. Mr. Carlson had told her that, once they had settled in Buenos Aires, she would have to be well dressed and well groomed at all times as a good many South Americans judged a man by the way his wife dressed.

Satisfied with the way her hair looked, Tasy debated trying to cover her freckles with makeup but decided against it. Andy didn't care if she had freckles. He thought they made her interesting-looking. All the makeup she would wear, she decided, was a touch of lipstick and a smidge of rouge.

Catalina came in with the dress she'd pressed while she was applying her lipstick. The housekeeper was still distraught. "Please, *Señorita,*" she begged. "I know what it is to be in love. I have buried two men. I know how much you are in love and want to be married, and I am very happy for you—but does it have to be so sudden? Why don't you postpone the wedding until tomorrow, at least for a few hours? The *Señora* is almost certain to be home by then."

"Why should I?" Tasy asked coldly. "I want out of here, understand?" She added less vehemently, "But I tell you what. When Mother does come home, tell her if she's ever in Buenos Aires, she must drop in and see us."

Catalina laid the dress on the bed. "I am only an employee, *Señorita.* It is not for me to say what you should or shouldn't do. But I do think that a mother should be at her daughter's wedding."

"Why?" Tasy asked. "Give me one good reason. What did my mother ever do for me except lug me all over the world, then stick me in that damn school in Switzerland between husbands and boy friends? Yes. And if she had her way, I'd probably still be there."

The housekeeper shrugged and left the room.

Tasy noticed the seam of one of her stockings was crooked and straightened it. Actually the school in Switzerland hadn't been too bad. She'd rather liked it. That is, she had liked it until she'd had the bad dream in Rome.

That one she remembered distinctly. It had happened, of all times, during the Easter holidays. Most of the other girls at school had been going home and she'd been dreading being alone when the letter from her mother had arrived containing a plane ticket, a few hundred dollars for pocket money, and, more important, the welcome news that her mother wanted her to spend her holidays with her and her most recent stepfather, a high-ranking French diplomat attached to the legation in Rome.

The visit had started out beautifully. Her mother and her stepfather had been living in an enormous suite in one of the better hotels catering to the international set. And the very first afternoon the three of them had eaten lunch at an outdoor café on the famous Via Veneto. She'd liked her new stepfather from the start. And later that afternoon her mother had laughed and said she hadn't realized how much she had filled out and that, now she'd become a young lady, they ought to dress her like one, and her mother had insisted on taking her shopping and had bought her several brand-new outfits of almost grown-up clothes, including a negligee and a baby-doll nightdress that would really bug out the eyes of the other girls when she returned to school.

She'd been in a glow all afternoon. It had been so

nice to feel wanted, to be a part of a family. The corners of Tasy's mouth tugged down as she refastened her garter. But that very first night, instead of staying with her or planning something that all of them could do, after tipping one of the bellboys, a rather good-looking boy named Luigi, perhaps five or six years older than she was, to look in on her from time to time to see if there was anything she wanted, her mother and father had gone to a dinner dance and party at one of the legations.

"You understand, darling," her mother had said. "It's good publicity for me. Besides, contract time is coming up. One of the most important of the new producers in Italy is going to be there. And none of these Italian broads have one damn thing I don't have."

Tasy supposed she shouldn't have reacted as she had, but a girl couldn't help how she felt. She'd bawled all through a lonely dinner served in the suite, because in Italy "nice" girls didn't dine out alone, not even in hotel dining rooms. Then after she'd eaten she'd looked out the windows and tried to read and had listened to the radio. She'd even drunk a small glass of wine, thinking it might make her feel better, and had kept right on blubbering.

And the next time the boy who had been assigned to keep an eye on her had knocked on the door to see if there was anything she wanted, he had brought a cheap box of candy with him and had said he was desolated to see the little *signorina* so unhappy and he, for one, was very happy to welcome her to Rome. And she had been so pleased and surprised that she had invited him in for a glass of wine and hadn't even protested when, before he left, he'd pulled her to him and kissed her hard on the mouth and run one of his hands over her bottom while he'd cupped one of her breasts with the other. In fact she had rather enjoyed it.

That was why, Tasy supposed, she'd dreamed what she had, the first of the really bad dreams she'd dreamed.

In her dream, as she'd dreamed it, after the boy had left, she had listened to the radio some more, and when she'd gotten bored with that, for want of something better to do, she'd gotten ready for bed. Then she had dreamed that shortly after eleven o'clock, when he had gotten off duty, Luigi had come back to the suite, and after he had let himself in with his pass key, he'd poured them both another glass of wine and they'd sat on the sofa in the living room and talked.

At first they'd talked mostly about motion pictures both of them had seen and what a good actress her mother was and how well Sophia Loren and Gina Lollobrigida were doing in the United States. Then when Luigi had said he thought it was because all Italian girls had such beautiful legs, perhaps because she wasn't used to drinking wine, or you did things in dreams you wouldn't think of doing any other time, she'd dreamed she'd said, "Oh, I don't know. Some American girls have pretty legs." And to prove it she'd opened her negligee and had pulled up the ruff of the baby-doll nightdress to show him how pretty her legs were before she'd remembered, too late to do anything about it, that she hadn't put on the matching bloomers. Not that, as she recalled, she'd been particularly embarrassed. In her dream it had all seemed very normal and natural and adult.

"Bella, bella, bella," Luigi had admired her.

Then, in her dream, he had picked her up and had

carried her into her bedroom and there hadn't been any kid stuff about what had happened after that. It might have been one of the underscored paragraphs out of her schoolmate's smuggled copy of *The Arabian Nights.*

One minute she had been sitting on the sofa in the living room fully clothed. The next she'd been lying crosswise on her bed, her negligee discarded, her new baby-doll pulled up over her breasts, and Luigi as naked as she was had been standing between her splayed and dangling legs, so close she could reach up and touch it, the rigid muscle thrusting out from between his thighs looming enormous in the half light shining through the crack of the door he'd only partially closed.

Tasy pressed one of her hands to her flushed cheeks. In her dream, she'd just lain looking up at him for a long time. Then when the tension had become almost unbearable, when she'd felt she was going to scream, she'd dreamed that she'd reached up her hand and had heard her own voice, sounding very mature and grown up, asking, "Well? What are you waiting for? Don't you like girls with freckles?"

"Si, si," Luigi had said. *"Con permesso, signorina."*

Then after he'd asked her permission, with her guiding and helping him, the bellboy's lowering bulk had blotted out what little light there was.

Tasy wiped her palm absently with a tissue, then found and lighted a cigarette. Even for a dream, the first in a series of similar dreams, it had been very embarrassing. Time after time she'd tried to wake up, but couldn't. In her dream she hadn't been able to find her way out of Luigi's arms or make him stop doing what he was to her, or had wanted him to. When she had been able to think coherently again, it had been almost morning and she'd looked up to see her mother standing beside the bed, brushing her damp hair away from her forehead, pretending to be concerned.

"What's the matter, baby?" her mother had asked her. "Are you sick?"

Even then she'd had to lie quietly for a long time, reorienting herself, the dream still so vivid she had expected the bed to erupt into motion again any moment, almost afraid to turn her head for fear she would see Luigi lying beside her, or, worse, spiral off into space making the remembered *ah ah aha ah ah* sounds in her throat. When she was able to speak, she'd said, "No. I'm not sick. I feel fine. I—just had a bad dream, that's all."

And she'd hated her mother ever since.

Tasy made a swipe at the buzzing fly that persisted in annoying her. But all that was in the past. Now not even her last bad dream mattered. And that hadn't been a dream. That had been a nightmare, with her knowing exactly what she was doing every minute.

Having the painting of herself and Brunnhilde and Sally altered had seemed such a good idea. She'd reasoned that Mrs. Harris would find it and, quarreling as they were, as jealous as she was of Mr. Harris, Mrs. Harris would raise holy hell and show the picture to their parents. And while Mr. and Mrs. Schilling and her mother wouldn't have been too perturbed, General Ti would blow his stack and lay down the law to Sally and the whole filthy business would come out in the confusion and when the dust had settled she would have Andy back again and everything would be as it had been with them.

But while it had worked out that way, it hadn't been exactly as she'd planned. Not that it made any difference. In another few minutes she would be married to Andy and wouldn't ever have to have any more dreams, or reason for having any.

Tasy repaired the tear stains in her makeup, then got up from the bench and slipped her wedding dress over her head. Well, it wasn't exactly a wedding dress, but it was white and new and looked good on her. She didn't think, even if she was home, her mother would mind her wearing it. Among a number of other things they had in common, they both wore the same size.

She checked the traveling case on the luggage rack to make certain that Catalina had put her traveling suit on top and had packed the things she would need for her honeymoon night in the capital and on the plane for Buenos Aires, then sat back on the vanity bench to wait for Brunnhilde and Herman.

She wished she knew what had happened to Sally. She'd told Mr. Harris the truth about that, too. Sally was her best friend, the only real girl friend she'd ever had. That was why it had hurt her so deeply when she and Andy had done what they had to her.

Tasy made premarital penance. But she hadn't been truthful about one thing. She'd known about Sally and Andy almost from the start. That's why she'd done what she had. They'd had guilt written all over their faces. Besides, on three separate occasions, she'd followed them when they'd sneaked away from the gang. Tasy snuffed her cigarette.

In her desperation, she'd even thought of killing Sally. That thought had occurred to her the afternoon she had seen Mrs. Harris take a funny-looking knife out of her purse and lay it on Mr. Harris' work table.

I'll fix that hot-pantsed little Chinese bitch, she'd thought. *I'll cut off her goddamn fringe.*

She'd even waited beside the pool for several nights

hoping to catch Sally alone. Then the night of the morning that Sally had turned up missing, she'd realized she couldn't do that to a girl with whom she had been as good friends as she and Sally had been. That was why she'd thrown the knife into the pool, then almost wet her bikini when Juan had fished it out with his skimmer.

A car horn beeped in front of the house. Catalina came into the room and closed and picked up the traveling case. "Señor Gottlieb and Señorita Schilling are here."

"I heard the horn," Tasy said. She pinned the small buckram shell with its length of white veiling to her hair. "Well, give Mother my best regards."

"What can I say?" the housekeeper said. *"Vaya con Dios, Señorita.* Go with God."

Tasy turned for a last look in the mirror and saw that the fly had finally landed. She thrust out a shell-pink palm and there was a satisfying squashing feel as she mashed the fly against the unyielding glass.

Abdul shouldn't have threatened to tell Mr. Harris. Nice men didn't threaten nice girls. She'd been through that nightmare before.

Chapter Twenty-one

The aged Mexican who acted as night watchman for the business block touched the brim of his battered black felt hat in respect as the two young *chinos* who worked for General Ti emerged from the front door of the building shortly before nine o'clock.

"You are working late tonight, *Señores.*"

"Yes. I guess you could say that," Harry Toy said.

He stood surveying the night scene as he took his

package of cigarettes from his pocket. The narrow street was alive with sound and teeming with curious tourists and local males out for a night on the town. The animated neon signs of the nightclubs and *cantinas* and cheap hotels blinked on and off with a dogged rhythm. The bilingual barkers standing in front of the clubs extolled the virtues of their shows and the thousand and one delights available to any male fortunate enough to pass through the brightly lighted doorways. The still night air was heavy with the smell of chiles and garlic and stale beer, the reek of antiseptics, and the cloying fragrance of unclad female flesh anointed with inexpensive perfumes.

Toy shook a cigarette from his package and put it in his mouth. "That's what the guy said."

"Said what?" Charlie Lee asked.

"'For God so loved the world, that he gave his only begotten Son, that whosoever believeth in Him should not perish, but have everlasting life.'"

Lee glanced at the other man sharply. "Not two in one night?"

"No," Toy said. "Merely thinking out loud. Just something I heard in a mission once." He offered his package of cigarettes to the watchman.

"Gracias," the old man said. "You are very kind, *Señor."* With Charlie Lee walking beside him, Toy walked down the crowded sidewalk for a few yards, then leaned against the corner of the building and sucked thoughtfully at the cigarette he lighted. "What are you going to do, Charlie?"

"I haven't made up my mind," Lee said.

"I have. I'm going to grab me a handful of jet and head back for 'Frisco in the morning. In a way I'm rather glad this happened. I want to see and smell some nice clean 'Frisco fog and feel the wind blowing down Geary Street. And maybe go down to Fisherman's Wharf and eat a mess of prawns, then grab a cab out to the ball park and watch Marichal throw a few. I'm up to here with perpetual sunshine and balmy tropical breezes. And tamales and enchiladas and bullfights."

Lee forced himself to laugh. "I'll buy that. The thing that puzzles me is why the old man is willing to throw away everything it's taken him two years to build."

"Conscience maybe," Toy said. "I don't think he's been too happy pushing the stuff. And now that this has happened, his kid getting herself in the mess she has, I suppose he has a feeling it's a form of retribution, that Buddha or Confucius, or whoever he burns his joss sticks to, is getting back at him."

Lee protested, "But as Guerrero pointed out this afternoon, the users are going to get it somewhere and they might as well buy it from us."

"Who's giving you an argument?" Toy said. "I'd sell my own mother a packet if she had the dough." He added philosophically, "But the old man should make out all right. He still has his import-export business. And even after giving us our cut on this last deal, plus a few grand for severance pay, he still has over eighty grand in that tin box he calls a safe." Toy pushed himself away from the building. "Well, see you around some time."

"Yes. Around," Lee said.

"If you ever are in 'Frisco look me up. Maybe I can cut you in on something."

"I'll do that."

Neither man offered to shake hands.

Lee watched Toy out of sight, then crossed to the other side of the narrow street and walked into a nightclub and sat in the booth in the front window.

The old man couldn't do this to him. Not only had Ti wriggled completely off the hook, but by his most recent action he'd put him in a very bad light with the party. If he had to go back to Peking and report he'd not only failed to get Ti, but the onetime general had turned legitimate and therefore was no longer vulnerable, *he* could be the one to wind up facing a firing squad.

A mildly pretty girl in a red dress came over to the booth and sat beside him. "How you like to buy Agata a dreenk, *chino?*"

Lee started to wave her away but changed his mind. If you refused to buy her a drink, one of the other girls in the club would replace her.

"Okay," Lee said. "Order whatever you want and tell the waiter to bring me a beer. But don't talk. I have some thinking to do."

"Whatever you say," the girl said as she signaled to one of the waiters. "But after we have a few drinks and I do my dance and you see how pretty I am, you like to come with me, no?" She pressed her knee against his. "I show you ver' good time for ten dollars."

Lee continued his study of the lighted window of General Ti's office. The shade was up. The old man was clearly visible as he performed his nightly ritual of changing the water in their cage, when feeding his lovebirds before leaving for home.

Lee had never felt quite so frustrated. If he'd known that the day was going to end like this, he'd have followed his first hunch and have taken off with the shipment before Ti had turned it over to Guerrero.

A waiter brought his beer and an anise for the girl, then picked up the bill Lee laid on the table and dropped a plastic chip in front of her.

Without relaxing the pressure of her knee, the girl

put the chip in the top of her other stocking, then raised her glass in a toast.

"*Salud.*"

"*Salud,*" Lee said absently.

It was, he supposed, a great honor to be a trusted agent in the disciplinary branch of the party. He'd worked hard to get where he was. Few men of his age rose that high. But when a man faced facts, the hours and the pay were lousy and he was forced to live under constant tension.

The general had given himself and Harry Toy their usual five percent of the transaction with Guerrero, plus two thousand dollars in severance pay. He had seven thousand dollars in his pocket. There were eighty-six thousand more in the safe that Ti couldn't bank before morning. He knew, but Ti didn't know he knew, the combination of the safe. And while ninety-three thousand dollars was only a fraction of the money that 25 kilos of uncut heroin would retail for north of the border, it was enough to take a man anyplace he might want to go.

He could even go to Paris. From what he'd heard and read, the French capital was quite a town.

Lee sipped at his beer. They were small things, he supposed, but the items he'd read in the local paper continued to bother him. There were, it seemed, three entirely different generations of Chinese. General Ti's. His. And this one in the making.

The China he'd known had changed in the short time he'd been on his current assignment. Now, according to the most recent news story he'd read, the rampaging youthful Red Guard of the great proletarian cultural revolution had decreed that all traditional holidays were to be abolished, no one would be permitted to grow flowers, keep birds, or collect stamps, and that only men over forty would be permitted to smoke or drink.

Lee lit a cigarette from the stub of the one he was smoking. He'd never had any desire to grow flowers, keep birds, or collect stamps, but he'd been a chain smoker since he was fifteen and he enjoyed a drink on occasion.

It all sounded way out to him.

The girl sitting beside him persisted in pressing her knee against his. "You like Agata, no? You like to buy her another drink?"

Lee laid another bill on the table. "Be my guest. And while you're at it, order me a double bourbon."

Pleased by the progress she hoped she was making, the girl smiled expansively. *"Si."*

Lee resumed his contemplation of the building across the street. The light in Ti's inner office had gone out. A few minutes later the big man emerged from the front door and waited patiently for the watchman to unlock the padlock on the gate of the fenced parking area in which the tenants of the building kept their cars.

His daughter's disappearance had hit Ti hard, physically as well as mentally. His normally perfectly fitting white suit coat looked too big for his massive frame. His shoulders sagged. He shuffled as he walked. He looked almost as old as the watchman.

"But what are you going to do about Sally?" Harry Toy had asked him.

And Ti had said, "What can I do? We've done all that can be done. Now all that is left is for me to put that ad in the paper in the morning and hope for the best."

Lee drank the bourbon the waiter brought him. It was in a sense ironic. He'd done what he'd been sent to do. He'd destroyed the virtue of Ti's daughter. He'd turned the girl into an addict. He'd even broken Ti. But not in the way the disciplinary council had decreed.

The party didn't want Ti shot in some dark alley. They wanted him to die slowly. They wanted to make an example of him, with full newspaper and wire-service coverage.

The girl sitting beside Lee attempted to make certain of the fee for services rendered that she hoped to earn by slipping the strap of her evening gown and exposing a *café-con-leche*-colored breast. "You like?"

"Very pretty," Lee said dryly. "And I understand they are very rare. Only two to a woman."

He had a decision to make. He had to make it fast. He could return to Peking and report he'd failed. He could take the money in the safe, row out to the ketch and warn the de Bravo woman to blow town, possibly waltz with the black-haired little broad a few more times, then do what Harry Toy had said he was going to do. Only he would head out in the other direction and, eventually, wind up in Paris. Or possibly Tangiers. He'd heard Tangiers was a wide-open town, and if and when he ran out of money, he ought to be able to tie in with some outfit who had need for a man with his particular talents.

"You come with Agata now?" the girl asked. "I don't dance for a half hour."

"Some other time," Lee said. "But not tonight."

To assuage any disappointment she might feel or loss of face she might suffer, and to avoid a possible scene that might draw attention to him, he covered what she was exposing with a ten dollar bill.

What difference did a few dollars make? He had eighty-six thousand of them waiting for him in a safe that could be opened with a nail file and no one guarding the safe but a pair of proscribed lovebirds.

Lee laughed rather grimly.

"Sometheeng is fonny?" the girl asked.

Lee sobered. "No. Not really."

He was taking a big step. He had been sent to get Ti. When he failed to return, someone would be sent to find out what happened to him. And once he left the club and crossed the narrow street, he was condemning himself to spend the rest of his life looking back over *his* shoulder.

Chapter Twenty-two

Ocho and *nueve* were *diecisiete* and carry *tres* came to *veinte*. Multiplied by *diez* made *doscientos*. Plus the profit on the champagne and the other drinks that the guests had ordered—Señor Córdoba totaled the figures he'd compiled and smiled, pleased by his own perspicacity. He hadn't missed it by far. Young Señor and Señora Carlson's wedding reception, to be paid for by the father of the groom, had netted him an excellent day's profit.

He almost wished it was Friday instead of Thursday. If this was tomorrow night, he could lock up and drive home and share his pleasure with Luiza. His pleased smile became resigned. With Luiza and Alberico and Cirilo and Paco and Eva and Fiorentina and Eduardo and Teresa and Juanito and Eustasio and Eustaquito. And since he'd been home two days before there was probably another blessing from God on its way. He hoped that *Dios* and His Holy Highness and Father Zamorra knew what they were doing. If it was true that a man's monument were his children, he had more *pocas estaturas* in his *casa* than most churches had stations of the cross.

He put his account book away, then looked over the top of his glasses to make certain, now they were drinking on their own again, that none of his familiars were in need of service. None of them seemed to be. He would give Paquita that. She was an excellent waitress.

Córdoba took off and folded his glasses and laid them on the back bar. It had been, he decided, for all of the haste involved, a very impressive wedding. He'd heard it said that all girls were beautiful on their wedding day. Now he believed it. While, admittedly, the child had a very attractive body, almost too lush for her years, he'd always thought the Lane girl rather plain-faced. But that hadn't been true after the Protestant priest of Señor Carlson's faith, in completing the marriage ceremony, had asked Tasy and Andy to join hands while he'd intoned:

"By the authority committed unto me as a minister of the Church of Christ, I declare that Andrew Carlson, Jr., and Ecstasy Lane are now husband and wife, according to the ordinance of God, and the law of this State: in the Name of the Father, and of the Son, and of the Holy Spirit. And whom God hath joined together, let no man put asunder."

Córdoba beamed at the memory. When the red-haired girl had lifted her veil to receive her first kiss as a wife, she had been truly beautiful, dewy, radiant, virginal young womanhood trembling on the brink of discovery. He hoped she and young Carlson would be very happy together.

Yawning, he scratched himself as youthful Señora Amapa came in by herself and gave her order to Paquita, then reached for a large liqueur glass and began to compile the gooey mixture of yellow and green Chartreuse, creme de cacao and creme de violette, and marschino and Benedictine and brandy, floated one on top of the other that Señora Amapa inevitably ordered.

As he was making the drink, the heavy-set Mexican woman sitting with her snoring husband at the table nearest the wall got up from her chair and came over to the bar and jabbed a work-worn finger in the general direction of the one-time Central American dictator's wife and asked in a conspiratorial whisper:

"She is Señora Lane?"

Señor Córdoba shook his head. "No, she is not *Señora.*" He attempted to be firm with the woman. *"Por favor.* How many times must I tell you I do not even know if Señora Lane will return this night? Why don't you and your husband be off and come back some other time?"

Blanca shook her head. "No. Another day we may not be so fortunate as to be able to borrow his cousin's truck. Now we have invested in the *gasolina,* we will wait. We have plenty of time."

Córdoba scowled at the woman's ample backside as she walked back to the table that she and her husband had occupied for the last four hours without ordering as much as one small bottle of beer between them. He hadn't the least idea who they were or what business they might have with Señora Lane. He was grateful they hadn't arrived until after the departure of the newlyweds. Such people could give a refined bar a bad name.

Paquita swished her skirts up to the service station and reached over the bar for a paper coaster. *"Un arco* for Señora Amapa."

Córdoba set the drink he'd prepared on her tray.

"One rainbow," he repeated the order, resigned.

One would think that a man would get used to such things, but seemingly he never did. He forced himself to think of the wedding. All in all, everything had gone well. The only even slightly discordant note had been Señora Ti keeping her lonely vigil at the *teléfono*. Córdoba smiled, genuinely pleased. Then about an hour ago the general had finally called and Señora Ti had driven into Acapulco to meet him. He hoped that the call had been good news, that the general had finally found Sally and he and his *Señora* were bringing her home.

There was a steady flow of lights on Costera Aleman and Gran Via Tropical and still more lights emanating from the homes and hotels rimming the bay and scattered through the dark hills. Here, though, on the beach, there were only the night and the stars and one lone kerosene lantern standing beside a slim Mexican girl patiently awaiting the return of her fisherman husband, lover, father.

Lee put the black attaché case and the brown paper sack on one of the thwarts of the rowboat, then pushed the boat into the water and rowed slowly but steadily towards the distant black hull of the ketch, feathering his oars from time to time to admire the phosphorescent silver drops of water dripping from the blades.

Now he'd committed himself, he felt fine. For the first time in his life he was his own man. He could see now why men defected. It was a heady feeling, this acceptance of independence, of being in a position to guide one's own destiny.

When he reached the ketch he made the boat fast to the landing platform, then climbed the short boarding ladder carrying the attaché case and the paper bag with him and descended the companionway stairs.

"Am I glad to see you!" Conchita de Bravo greeted him. "I'm almost out of my mind. When you did show up I was afraid it might be the police."

"I'm sorry," Lee apologized. He set the attaché case and the paper bag on the table. "I tried to get out here a half dozen times, but the old man hasn't let me out of his sight for the past twenty-four hours."

"What's in the bag?"

"Food for you. Some *tacos* and cold beer and a paper carton of *frijoles.*"

The nurse tore open the bag. "And can I use them. I haven't had anything to eat since I came out here last night." She spoke through a mouthful of chicken *tacos*. "Has Ti cracked yet?"

"Not yet," Lee said. He told the nurse the story he'd decided on. "And I don't think he's going to unless more pressure is put on him."

"How can you do that?"

"By beating the truth out of young Carlson. And if that doesn't work I'll drop Sally on his doorstep."

"Now wait just a moment, Colonel," Conchita said. "I think you ought to know that—"

"That such a direct attack will be risky?" Lee cut her short. "Everything we do in our line of work is a calculated risk." He opened two bottles of beer and gave one of them to the nurse. "You knew that when you accepted this assignment."

"I know," Conchita admitted, "but—"

"But because what I intend to do is risky," Lee said, "your part in the assignment is over. When you finish eating I want you to row back to shore and pack your things and get out of Acapulco."

"I'll be glad to," Conchita said. "I sat in this stinking cabin all last night and all of today afraid that something had gone wrong and the harbor police would pop down the companionway any minute. And I don't want any part of a Mexican jail. They're as bad as those we have in Cuba."

Carrying the bottle of beer with him, Lee walked into the forward cabin and looked at the girl sitting on the bunk, then back at the nurse who had followed him as far as the doorway and asked, sharply:

"What happened to her?"

Conchita shrugged. "I tried to tell you. She knows."

"Knows what?"

"Everything, including the fact we got her the way she is to get her to hold still for the needle."

"Who told her?"

"I did," Conchita admitted uneasily. "I'm sorry, but it just sort of slipped out. I didn't think anyone could possibly be as innocent as she was pretending to be."

Lee looked back at the girl on the bunk. Even in the torment she was enduring, rocking back and forth on the bunk, hugging herself with both arms, her agonized black eyes stared back at him defiantly.

"Don't you dare touch me," she said thickly. "And don't try to shoot any more of that stuff into my arm. Because if you do I'll kill you. I don't know how, but I will."

"How long since she's had a fix?" Lee asked.

"That's part of what I've been trying to tell you," Conchita said. "Not since last night. Not since she found out what we've been doing to her. She's been writhing around on that bunk and crawling on the floor and on the ceiling ever since, but she won't let me fix her. In the brief intervals when she's been able to talk lucidly, she claims she's going to cure herself—

cold turkey."

Lee studied the girl on the bunk with clinical interest. It was almost unbelievable what a three-month addiction to heroin could do to a healthy, wholesome teenager.

The Ti girl's exposed flesh had the waxen pallor of an addict. Her face looked old and drawn and haggard. The sheen was gone from her normally glossy black hair. She looked as if every nerve in her body were bleeding. As she sat rocking back and forth on the bunk, she alternately hugged herself in an attempt to ease the cramps that were convulsing her vital organs and brushed frantically at the imagined ants or worms she thought were crawling over her.

Jesus H. Christ, Lee thought. *Can't anyone do anything right any more?*

The Ti girl wasn't any use to him the way she was. About all he could do now was sedate her heavily enough to keep her from going completely mad until he could get out of Acapulco.

"You shouldn't have told her," he said.

"I know that now," Conchita admitted.

"Have you anything that will sedate her?"

"Yes. At least temporarily. Also a spare hypo." The nurse explained, "She kicked the other one out of my hand while I was trying to fix her so I could get some sleep."

Lee walked into the head and used the facility without bothering to close the door. "Get it. You can hold her while I fix her. And make it a double dose. I don't give a damn if the little bitch ever comes to. It might be better that way."

Standing where he was he could see the sky through the propped open hatch of the head. In a way he disagreed with Harry Toy. He liked sunny days and balmy nights and skies filled with stars. Perhaps he wouldn't go to either Paris or Tangiers. There were a number of small countries and islands in and off the coast of Central and South America where a man could live out his life very comfortably on the amount of money he had in the attaché case.

He tugged up the zipper of his fly and walked over to the built-in bunk where Conchita was waiting with a filled syringe. "You hold her while I fix her."

The nurse wrestled the protesting girl flat on the bunk, then sat on her legs and held her upper body while Lee lifted one of her arms and attempted to find a vein. Finding one he liked he bent over the bunk to prick it with the point of the needle, then straightened slowly as a male voice coming from the open door of the head asked, almost conversationally, "If I'm not being too presumptuous, Comrade Colonel, may I ask what you intend to do with that needle?"

Charlie Lee swiveled his head as painfully as he'd straightened, wondering how he could ever have thought that Ti looked like an old man. With his long black hair plastered to his head, barefoot, wearing a pair of sodden linen slacks instead of a loin cloth, his magnificent upper body, corded with muscles, dripping salt water, the big Manchu looked more like a Sumo wrestler of the third badge than he did like a former general or an Acapulco businessman.

"Where did you come from?" Lee asked.

Ti tested the sharpness of the knife he was holding against the flat surface of one of his thumbs and a thin red line appeared almost immediately. "That should be obvious, Comrade Colonel. After following you to the beach, I swam out here, then came in through the hatch on the head."

Lee's hand moved across his own chest towards the

butt of the gun in his shoulder holster. It stopped as a second male voice said, "I don't think I would if I were you, Charlie."

Lee glowered at Harry Toy. "You lied to me. You said you were going to San Francisco."

Toy shrugged. "I am. What's to keep me here? But when the general asks will I work for a few more hours, I figure I owe him that much."

Conchita stopped struggling with Sally and got to her feet. "Oh, no. This wasn't supposed to happen. I didn't bargain for anything like this. Ti was supposed to be in custody when he found out about his kid."

Toy had stepped inside the forward cabin leaving the doorway open. Her crumpled uniform rustling as she ran, the nurse ran for the dubious safety of the main cabin and stopped as Mrs. Ti stepped into the doorway that Toy had just quitted.

"Were you going somewhere, Miss?"

Her hair was slightly wind-blown. There was a big water stain on her dress where a dripping oar had splashed it, but the Russian woman's voice was as soft and well modulated as if she was standing in the ancestral drawing room she'd never seen, asking if a guest preferred sugar or lemon in her tea.

Sally got up from the bunk and ran to the woman in the doorway. "Oh Mother. I'm so ashamed."

The Russian woman held her for a moment in the universal understanding of all mothers. "It's all right, baby. Everything is going to be all right now. We'll work out everything some way. Can you walk?"

Too filled with emotion to speak, the teenager bobbed her head.

"That's our girl," Mrs. Ti said. She held out her hand and Harry Toy put the gun he was holding into it. "Now you go along with Mr. Toy, darling. He'll row you to shore and wait with you in the car. And Mother and Father will be with you in a few minutes. We won't be long."

"Not long," General Ti promised.

Chapter Twenty-three

The rain came early that evening. Shortly after eleven o'clock a line squall swept in off the bay and drenched the enclave with torrents of water. It rained hard for fifteen minutes. Then the wind died, the water soaked into the sand, the sky cleared and the stars came out again and everything was as it had been before.

At eleven-thirty Harris decided if Sonia intended to come home she would have been home by now. When he had left Acapulco that afternoon, the arrangement had been that Mrs. Meier would phone Elsie as soon as Sonia woke up and Elsie would take Sonia to her apartment and attempt to convince her that what had happened wouldn't mean anything to their future relationship, that he blamed himself even more than he did her.

Then, perhaps because of the lateness of the hour, Elsie had decided it might be best for Sonia to wait until morning before she came home. But in that case, why didn't Elsie phone him?

Harris scowled at the phone on the bar. Even Mrs. Ti had finally gotten her call and the Russian woman had taken off as if she'd been shot out of a gun.

Things, he reflected, had a way of working themselves out. If young Carlson had been having an affair with and had impregnated the Chinese girl, it was just as well that the general hadn't found her in time to bring her home to see him being married to Tasy.

The babble of conversation, the slap of cards, and the tinkle of chips was making his head ache. His eyes smarted. His throat was raw. He felt as if he hadn't slept in a week.

Harris signaled to Córdoba. "Give me another double, please. And if there should be a phone call for me. I'll be out by the pool."

"*Si, Señor,*" Córdoba said.

Harris picked his fresh drink from the wood and walked out into the night. The recent rain had drenched the pads of the chairs on the flagging. He walked the length of the pool intending to sit on the anchored end of the diving board and saw it was occupied.

"Hi," Cara Lane greeted him.

"Hi," Harris said as he sat on the board beside her. "That wouldn't be a drink in that glass?"

"As it so happens, yes."

"May I have it?"

"Of course."

Harris gave the actress his glass. She emptied it, then handed it back to him. "As the man said, I needed that." She explained, "I walked down to lift a few. In fact I intended to get stinking. Then for some reason I couldn't go in."

Harris neither liked nor disliked Cara Lane. There were times when she rather disturbed him. She always reminded him of a pretty little alley cat who, having been groomed and coached by experts, had been even more surprised than they when she had been awarded a blue ribbon for feline perfection. He asked, "Since when have you been bashful about climbing up on a bar stool?"

She made a small gesture with one hand. "Please. Don't give me a rough time, Harris. Not tonight. I just flew back from Mexico City. And I got the goddamn part. Don't ask me how. You know. Anyway, it looks like it could be a come-back. The script isn't bad. The money is good. I've finally landed a lead in an Aztec Maypole epic. I'm even getting top billing."

"Good," Harris said.

"I felt pretty good myself," the actress admitted. "Until I got back half an hour ago and my housekeeper told me that Tasy was married this afternoon."

"I went to the wedding."

"Whose idea was it? His or hers?"

"That I wouldn't know. But I think the bridegroom's father had a large part in the decision."

Cara laid her hand on Harris' forearm. "Tell me about it."

Harris was as inept as most men in describing a wedding. "Well, Tasy wore a white dress. One of yours, I imagine. Young Gottlieb was Andy's best man and Brunnhilde was Tasy's bridesmaid. Oh, yes. And there was a *mariachi* band that played the wedding march and 'Oh Promise Me' and somehow managed to make both of them sound like 'La Paloma.'"

"Did the kid seem happy?"

"I'd say, no pun intended, ecstatically so."

"How did she look?"

"Beautiful."

"Did she wear a veil?"

"Yes."

"She would."

Harris waited for Cara to amplify the implication she'd made. Instead she said quietly, "Well, I suppose I'm very happy for her. It only takes one guy, if he happens to be the right one. I found one once, her father. It was my tough luck he died when I was about her age, less than a year after she was born."

"She told me about him," Harris said. "That is, she said he left her a lot of money that will come to her when she's nineteen."

The actress shook her head. "No. I just made that up, to go along with the rest of her dream world. Except on pay days her father never had more than five dollars in his pocket at any given time. He was just a part-time stock boy and checker in a supermarket in Van Nuys." She explained, "That's a small town in the San Fernando Valley, a few miles out of L.A."

"I know where it is," Harris said.

Cara put a cigarette between her lips and waited for him to light it. "I even had to wash her diapers in one of those drop-a-quarter-in-the-slot laundromats. Not that it mattered. We were both kids ourselves and I was crazy about the guy." She added, "And Tasy does have money coming to her. While I was making it big," the actress was deliberately vague about it, "before that trouble in Malibu, I put a hundred grand in a trust fund and let a lawyer damn near pound me to death to set up the fund so it would look like it came from her father." She filled her lungs with smoke and exhaled. "Oh, I had as good a time as he did. By then there'd been a lot of men, talent agents, casting directors, head cameramen, producers, associate producers. You know something, Harris?"

"What?"

"Someone ought to do a documentary about what the dewy-eyed little hopefuls in Hollywood have to go through to make it big in the business. I even know one producer who is too busy to do his own spade work. When he spots a bit player or some beauty queen he thinks could be built into star or feature-player material, he has an assistant who takes her to Tahoe or Vegas to calibrate her rate of feedback on a Beauty Rest to make certain it's worth his while to invite her to spend a weekend with him in Palm Springs."

Harris studied the actress' face. She was obviously having a difficult time maintaining the ultrasophisticated, brittle, veneer that, along with her beauty and talent, had made her one of the all-time highest-paid box-office attractions.

"Do you want me to get you another drink, Cara?" he asked her.

"No," she said. "That's not where I hurt. I just want to talk to someone. Someone I can trust. Have you ever noticed anything strange about Tasy?"

"In what way?"

"Do you remember the picture June Lange made some years ago—*The Three Faces of Eve?*"

"Yes."

"Well, that's how it is with Tasy. And while I don't know why, I think I know when it started. About five years, in Rome. You see, the kid lives in two worlds. And the thing that worries me is I've never been able to decide if she is kidding herself or if she really doesn't know when she slips from one into the other."

Cara smoked in silence for a moment "Like when I got the letter from the woman who ran the school in Switzerland. She was very nice about it. But she claimed the reason she was expelling the kid and shipping her back to me was because Tasy had become a bad example to the other girls. She claimed that while she had no actual proof, and Tasy denied it she was fairly certain that Tasy, as she phrased it, had been 'enjoying frequent and repeated sexual congress with the school's twenty-five-year-old ski instructor, the older brother of one of her classmates, one of the tellers in the Swiss bank through which I was paying her tuition, and various and sundry adult males.'"

"How old was she then?" Harris asked.

"Thirteen," Cara said. "But her age didn't make any difference. The women in our family mature early. And if I'm right about this thing, the kid was born ten thousand years old. Naturally when she arrived, I raised holy hell with Tasy. But she claimed it was all a lot of lies. She said she had never permitted any man, or boy, to be intimate with her, and that she never intended to until she met a man she really loved and was married to him. She said that the headmistress and the other girls at the school were just jealous of her because she had prettier clothes and a bigger allowance than they did and was the daughter of a famous motion-picture star."

"Did you believe her?"

"I didn't have any choice. She hates me, but I like her. After all, she's my kid. She came out of me. I brought her into this stinking world. So I said we wouldn't say anything more about it and I enrolled her in the local high school. And she got along fine. She made good grades. She liked her teachers. They liked her. Because we lived on the beach and I had a big house and a pool, there were kids in and out of it all the time. Raising hell. Frying hamburgers. Grilling hotdogs. Drinking cases of soft drinks. Playing Beatles and Herman's Hermits and Tijuana Brass records until I thought I'd go out of my mind.

"Yes. And petting, too. And because of the letter, and because I didn't want her to wind up as sick that way as I am, I kept my eyes on the kid. But while she went pretty far with a couple of the punks, so far with one of them they both had to wash their dirty little hands, it was, after all, just kid stuff. Besides, as the psychoanalyst I was going to at the time pointed out, all young people go through a curious stage and under the current teen set-up, if a girl wants to be popular and run with the crowd, she can't be too prudish about such things."

The actress dropped her cigarette on the flagging and ground out the sparks with the toe of one of her sixty-dollar alligator shoes. "So I went along with the bit. And I don't think she ever did, not with any of the boys. They belonged in her normal world, a world in which a girl, even if her mother was a tramp, only went so far and no farther until she fell in love with a guy and they were married."

"I think Tasy is in love with Andy," Harris said. "In fact I know she is. She told me so."

"Good," Cara said. "Good. I'm glad to hear that. Because after she had been home about a year, I woke up early one morning and started out on the lanai to get the paper and there my darling little red-haired daughter was, stripped right down to her freckles, spread-eagled on one of the chaises, servicing the twenty-year-old punk who serviced the swimming pool. And she didn't need a road map. She'd been over the route before. She'd been over it a lot of times."

Harris thought back to last night. It was the identical story Tasy had told him. Only in her version of the telling, her mother had been on the chaise. He asked, "What did you do?"

The actress shrugged. "What could I do? Beat her? Send her to a school for delinquent girls? I'll tell you what I did. I didn't do a damn thing. I didn't even let them know I'd seen them. Because, and that's the reason why I'm telling you all this, why I mentioned

The Three Faces of Eve, I still don't know if in that twisted little mind of hers, on that dark sound stage behind the mental door she seemingly opens and closes at will, outside of the natural physical stimuli and, I presume, eventually climactic, she fully realized what she was doing."

"What made you think that?"

"Because all the time I stood watching, she just lay there with her eyes closed and the same far-away expression on her face she'd had on her face that morning in Rome when she told me she'd had a bad dream."

Cara put another cigarette in her mouth and waited for Harris to light it. "That's what she said. I knew then. I *had* to know. But I didn't want to believe it. I wanted her life to be different from mine. I wanted her to have an entirely different set of values.

"'What's the matter, baby?' I asked her. 'Are you sick?' and she told me, 'No. I'm not sick. I feel fine. I just had a bad dream.' This with Henri and me gone all night, her face burning with fever, that beautiful body of hers covered with dried sweat, her new negligee and nightdress wadded into a ball under one of the pillows, and her bed looking as if a herd of young bull elephants had used it to audition for a remake of *The Return of Tarzan.*"

"But you didn't do anything then, or that morning in Malibu?"

"No. Nothing except change hotels and pool services. You see, even if I have never been able to make her understand, in my own way I love Tasy. I'd do anything in the world for her. And I didn't want to lose her entirely."

Harris hesitated, asked, "And that business in Malibu?"

"What do you know about that?"

"Only what was in the newspapers at the time. That the Malibu police and the State of California claimed you shot one of your lovers because you caught him with another woman. That you escaped being indicted because all the evidence was circumstantial and the studios had enough muscle to enable you to make a deal."

The actress got up from the diving board. "That's about the way it was. But I didn't shoot the guy. I loved him. I liked him better than any other man I'd ever met since Tasy's father died. We'd even talked of getting married. Even if he was a Vegas hood. Even if he did have a bad habit of sleeping with his gun on the night table. No. There'd been another woman in the bed. But Steve had been dead for an hour when I found him. And it took me almost that long again to get up the courage to call the police."

Harris had risen with her. "Now just one minute, Cara. You're not inferring—"

"I never infer," the actress said. "I'm just pointing out that I have a problem." She started for the lighted doorway of the clubhouse, then turned back. "Or maybe I'm merely being over protective. After all, it has been some hours since I signed my new contract. And as Tasy so kindly pointed out to General Ti yesterday afternoon, I get a little wacky if I go too long without attention."

She made a graceful full-arm gesture that included both the northern and southern hemispheres. "On the other hand, let's be honest about this thing. While there are millions of women out there, snug and smug in their unsullied beds, who probably wouldn't agree with me, and I certainly don't mean to be sacrilegious about it, with the instinct to mate as fundamental as it is, the basic source of all life, there have been times when I've lain in a man's arms, even in the arms of a stranger, and have felt a lot closer to God than I ever have in any church."

Chapter Twenty-four

Harris started to follow Cara Lane into the clubhouse, then changed his mind and walked around the end of the diving board, then up the wet winding black-topped private road that led past his house, skirting the puddles of water left by the recent rain.

He'd had all the whiskey and talk and raw emotion he could take for one day. There was so much he didn't know, might never know. But as corny and overused as the expression might be, that was the way life was.

In that one major respect, living differed sharply from any of the creative arts. You could paint a picture or write a book or sing a song or play an instrument and create the mood you wanted, lead up to practically any denouement you might have in mind. But life didn't turn out that way. Once the cosmic wheels started to turn, man had little to say about his ultimate destination. Seldom, if ever, was he permitted to see behind the scenes, and it didn't seem to make much difference if he crawled or walked or ran. At times life could be very rewarding. Other times the joke was on you. You were penalized right from the start merely for having the colossal effrontery of having poked your head out of your mother's womb.

He walked around a puddle of water in the road. He reached the foot of the short flight of stone steps leading up to the front patio and hesitated as a pair of car headlights turned off the Acapulco road.

The car disappointed him. It wasn't Sonia's Toyota. When it got close enough he could see it was General Ti's black Cadillac. Ti slowed the car to keep from splashing him, then braked to a stop and said cordially:

"Good evening, Mr. Harris." Ti indicated the girl sitting beside himself and Mrs. Ti. "Because I know you are concerned and were put to considerable inconvenience on her account, I want you to be one of the first to know that Mrs. Ti and I have found Sally."

"Good," Harris said sincerely. He rested his hands on the rolled-down window of the car as he looked into the dimly lighted interior. "Are you all right, honey?"

Her black eyes enormous in her abnormally pale face, a tic twitching one corner of her mouth, but sitting ramrod erect between her parents, the teenager said, "Yes. I'm quite all right now. And thank you for your concern, Mr. Harris." She hesitated briefly, and added, "Mother and Father tell me that Tasy and Andy were married this afternoon."

"That's right."

"How nice," the Chinese girl said. "I—hope they will be very happy."

Harris amended his thoughts of a few minutes ago. A man might not be in complete control of his life, but he could guide it. And in the business of living, as in everything else, class told. Sally might, or might not, be carrying Andy's child. But if she was, no one but her and her parents would ever know. And that could be taken care of.

General Ti said, "It would be a pleasure to prolong this conversation, Mr. Harris. But Mrs. Ti and I must get this child of ours to bed." He corrected himself. "I mean our very grown-up young woman of whom we are very proud." For the first time since Harris had known the man, rather awkwardly, but determinedly, the one-time general in the People's Army of China essayed a salutation in the tongue of his adopted country. *"Buenas noches, Señor."*

Harris inclined his head, *"Señor, Señora, Señorita."* He added, "And a special good night to you, Sally. While your father and I were talking yesterday, he said you had always spoken very highly of me. And I want you to know I feel the same way about you. You are one of the nicest and prettiest young women I've ever met, along with being one of my very best students. And when you marry, whoever gets you is going be a very fortunate young man."

Mrs. Ti reached across her daughter and her husband and rested one of her long-fingered, finely boned, capable hands on the back of one of Harris' hands for a moment. "What a lovely thing to say. And I hope that you and Mrs. Harris will always be as happy as General Ti and I are tonight."

"Señor Ti," the general corrected her gently.

Harris watched the car drive down the hill, stop briefly in front of the clubhouse, then drive on to the Ti home. He appreciated the sentiment, but it could be that Sonia wasn't ever coming home again. The only compelling factor stronger than fear was love. In a normal marital relationship the only thing stronger than love was pride. And it could well be through circumstance, and his own foolishness, he had maneuvered Sonia into a state of mind in which she felt that she couldn't face him.

The house had never seemed larger or so empty. Harris washed and dried the few dishes in the sink. Then, turning out all of the lights but one as he went, he walked through the house to the bedroom he and

Sonia had shared, and sat on the edge of the bed, holding his head in his hands, the all-enveloping silence magnifying the night noises outside the window. The tree frogs and the cicadas had never sounded louder or so shrill. The slap of the surf on the beach was like the pounding of drums. He'd never felt so helpless, or alone.

It had been a long day. Señor Córdoba was tired. It was sad, but true. He was no longer young and days like the one just past took a lot out of a man. While Pepe and Juan piled the chairs on top of the tables and Paquita and Juan's wife gathered up the last of the glasses and rinsed them, he unfolded his glasses and put them on, then opened his account book and added the 192 *pesos* in cash that Señora Lane had requested of him to her monthly running account.

It seemed like a lot of money to pay for the return of a small blue purse that couldn't have cost more than 40 *pesos* when it had been purchased. Then, who knew? There could have been something of value in the purse to cause Señora Lane to be willing to pay that much reward for its return.

Strangely, though, he hadn't seen anything that looked valuable when Señora Lane had emptied the purse on the bar. All it contained were the usual things women kept in purses. Still, 192 *pesos* was the amount the heavy-set woman had mentioned and after a few minutes of earnest conversation between them Señora Lane had paid the sum without quibbling.

He returned his account book to its niche, then saw that his employees had finished their work and were standing in front of the bar.

"Will there be anything else tonight, *patrón?*" Pepe asked.

Córdoba glanced around the room. Everything seemed to be in order. "No," he said. "You and Paquita and Juan and Lupe may go now." He added expansively, "And because all of you have worked so well today there will be a little something extra in your envelopes at the end of the week."

"Gracias, patrón," Paquita smiled.

Seeing something on the floor on her side of the bar, the young woman stooped to retrieve it.

They are pretty, Córdoba thought. Now that he had fully considered the matter he was beginning to change his mind about insisting that Paquita wear either a *camisa* or a bra. As she had told her husband, if God had not meant for her to have breasts he would have made her a man. Then, too, since she had begun to wait on the tables in the bar, his gross sales had gone up twenty percent. The older male residents of Rancho Paraíso had begun to start drinking earlier, were drinking more, and staying later. Only *Dios* himself knew how much each of her purple-flowered little pretties was worth in his cash register.

The young woman laid the object she'd picked from the floor on the bar and tried to read the name on the envelope. "Señora Lane," she succeeded.

"Gracias," Córdoba smiled. "It must have fallen from the lost purse that was returned to her this evening. I will give it to the *Señora* in the morning."

He watched the four young people leave the bar and begin the long walk up the beach to their homes, then poured himself a small glass of *aguardiente* and carried it around the bar and sat at one of his own tables to unwind before he locked up for the night and retired to his lonely cot in the service room behind the bar.

All in all it had been a good day. He'd made a

substantial profit. General Ti had stopped in briefly to inform him that his daughter had been returned to the bosom of her family. He was especially pleased by the way that Señora Lane had reacted to her daughter's wedding. She had listened intently to every word as he had described the ceremony from the *mariachi* band playing the wedding march to the tender moment when, after the Protestant priest had pronounced the two youngsters *marido* and *esposa,* her daughter had lifted her veil to receive her husband's kiss.

"Did she really seem to like the guy?" she'd asked him.

"Si, Señora," he'd told her. He'd tried to think of some way to describe how the bride had looked. "She could have been the Virgin of Guadalupe when she gave her heart to our Lord."

"Well, I doubt if I'd go that far," Señora Lane had said. Then, looking at her recovered blue purse, the *Señora* had said something that still puzzled him. "Did you ever play baseball, Córdoba?"

"No, *Señora,*" he'd been truthful with her. "When I was still young enough for so strenuous a game, I dived from La Quebrada."

"But you are familiar with the rules?"

"Si."

"How many strikes does a batter get?"

"Three strikes, *Señora,*" he'd informed her. "And that doesn't count foul tips."

"And would you say the same rule applies whether the player is a boy or a girl?"

"Señora," he had said, patient with her feminine lack of knowledge concerning sporting events. "What possible difference could that make? A rule is a rule."

"Okay," Señora Lane had replied. "That's the way

I'm going to play it. And if young Carlson remembers to take his vitamins, who knows? Maybe this is the pitch. Maybe the kid has just hit the big one out of the park."

Córdoba finished his drink and yawned, then realizing he'd carried the envelope Paquita had found on the floor to the table with him, he examined it incuriously.

It was merely an empty envelope addressed to Señora Lane, with a shopping list on the back. Except for her signature on a check it was the first time that Córdoba had ever seen a sample of Señora Lane's hand writing. It was surprisingly schoolgirlish for so *famosa* a *cinematografa* star. But then so was the list she'd compiled. The *Señora* had reminded herself to buy:

>2 lbs chocolates
>New Herb Alpert L.P.
>bobby pins
>tube of freckle bleach
>tampons
>Midol
>new bikini

Córdoba crumpled the envelope in his hand. It was obviously unimportant, not worth returning to the *Señora*. Yawning, he dropped the envelope into the trash can, then rinsed his empty glass and set it on the drain board and began to lock up for the night.

Harris was bending over to unlace his shoes when he heard the sound of the motor. It sounded like Sonia's Toyota. Headlights swept the house as the car turned into the carport. There was the sound of a car door opening and closing and a moment later the front door chimes filled the house.

In the hope Sonia might come home, Harris hadn't turned off the patio light. Every shining honey-colored hair combed carefully into place, the tic tugging at one corner of her mouth even more pronounced than Sally's had been, looking a little like a frightened puppy who had been bad, and kicked, but who was determined to crawl back to its master, Sonia was standing on the far side of the sliding screen door.

"My name is Sonia von Erlac Harris," the blonde girl said. "The Elsie Fillmore Agency sent me. And all I do is model."

Harris slid back the sliding screen door and held out his hand. "Come in, Mrs. Harris. Please."

THE END

Day Keene Bibliography
(1903-1969)

This is Murder, Mr. Herbert and Other Stories (1948)
Framed in Guilt (1949; published in UK as Evidence Most Blind, 1949)
Farewell to Passion (1951; reprinted as The Passion Murders, 1951)
Love Me—and Die (1951; as by Keene, collaboration with Gil Brewer)
My Flesh is Sweet (1951)
To Kiss, or Kill (1951)
About Doctor Ferrel (1952)
Home is the Sailor (1952)
Hunt the Killer (1952)
If the Coffin Fits (1952)
Naked Fury (1952)
Wake Up to Murder (1952)
Mrs. Homicide (1953)
Strange Witness (1953)
The Big Kiss-Off (1954)
Death House Doll (1954)
His Father's Wife (1954; reprinted as by "Daniel White," 1970)
Homicidal Lady (1954)
Joy House (1954)
Notorious (1954)
Sleep With the Devil (1954; reprinted in Australia as Sin With the Devil, 1955)
There Was a Crooked Man (1954; revised 1963)
The Dangling Carrot (1955)
Who Has Wilma Lathrop? (1955)
Bring Him Back Dead (1956; revised 1963)
Flight by Night (1956)
Murder on the Side (1956)
It's a Sin to Kill (1958; reprint of Dead Man's Tide, 1953, as by William Richards)
Passage to Samoa (1958)
Dead Dolls Don't Talk (1959)
Dead in Bed (1959; Johnny Aloha series)
Moran's Woman (1959)

So Dead My Lovely (1959)
Take a Step to Murder (1959)
Too Black for Heaven (1959)
Too Hot to Hold (1959)
The Brimstone Bed (1960)
Chautauqua (1960; with Dwight Vincent)
Miami 59 (1960)
Payola (1960; Johnny Aloha series)
World Without Women (1960; with Leonard Pruyn)
Seed of Doubt (1961)
Bye, Bye Bunting (1963)
L.A. 46 (1964; published in UK as City of Angels, 1964)
Carnival of Death (1965)
Chicago 11 (1966)
Acapulco G.P.O. (1967)
Guns Along the Brazos (1967)
Wild Girl (1969; reprint of 1952 edition as by Lewis Dixon)
Live Again, Love Again (1970)
League of the Grateful Dead and Other Stories: Vol. 1 (2010)
We Are the Dead and Other Stories: Vol. 2 (2010)
Death March of the Dancing Dolls and Other Stories: Vol. 3 (2011)
The Case of the Bearded Bride and Other Stories: Vol. 4 (2013)
A Corpse Walks in Brooklyn and Other Stories: Vol. 5 (2014)
Homicide House and Other Stories: Vol. 6 (2015)

As Lewis Dixon

Wild Girl (1952; reprinted 1969 as by Keene)

As William Richards

Dead Man's Tide (1953; reprinted as It's a Sin to Kill as by Keene, 1958)

As Daniel White

Southern Daughter (1954; reprinted as by Keene, 1967)
His Father's Wife (1970; originally published as by Day Keene, 1954)

Born Gunard R. Hjerstedt in Chicago on March 28, 1904, Day Keene became an actor in repertory theater in the early 1920's. When his actor friends decided to try film, he instead turned to writing, and during the 1930's was a principal writer for the "Little Orphan Annie" radio show, as well as contributing to the pulps. After he moved to the west coast of Florida, he began writing paperback originals in the late 1940's, mostly fast-paced crime stories. By the 1960's, he had abandoned mysteries for mainstream novels. He died in North Hollywood on January 9, 1969.

BLACK GAT BOOKS offers the best in reprint crime fiction from the 1950s-1970s. New titles appear every month, and each book is sized to 4.25" x 7", just like they used to be. Collect them all.

Harry Whittington · A Haven for the Damned #1 ·
Charlie Stella · Eddie's World #2
Leigh Brackett · Stranger at Home #3
John Flagg · The Persian Cat #4
Malcolm Braly · Felony Tank #6
Vin Packer · The Girl on the Best Seller List #7
Orrie Hitt · She Got What She Wanted #8
Helen Nielsen · The Woman on the Roof #9
Lou Cameron · Angel's Flight #10
Gary Lovisi · The Affair of Lady Westcott's Lost Ruby / The Case of the Unseen Assassin #11
Arnold Hano · The Last Notch #12
Clifton Adams · Never Say No to a Killer #13
Ed Lacy · The Men From the Boys #14
Henry Kane · Frenzy of Evil #15
William Ard · You'll Get Yours #16
Bert & Dolores Hitchens · End of the Line #17
Noël Calef · Frantic #18
Ovid Demaris · The Hoods Take Over #19
Fredric Brown · Madball #20
Louis Malley · Stool Pigeon #21
Frank Kane · The Living End #22
Ferguson Findley · My Old Man's Badge #23
Paul Connolly · Tears are for Angels #24
E. P. Fenwick · Two Names for Death #25
Lorenz Heller · Dead Wrong #26
Robert Martin · Little Sister #27
Calvin Clements · Satan Takes the Helm #28
Jack Karney · Cut Me In #29
George Benet · The Hoodlums #30
Jonathan Craig · So Young, So Wicked #31
Edna Sherry · Tears for Jessie Hewitt #32
William O'Farrell · Repeat Performance #33
Marvin Albert · The Girl With No Place to Hide #34
Edward S. Aarons · Gang Rumble #35
William Fuller · Back Country #36
Robert Silverberg · The Killer #37
William R. Cox · Make My Coffin Strong #38
A. S. Fleischman · Blood Alley #39
Harold R. Daniels · The Girl in 304 #40
William H. Duhart · The Deadly Pay-Off #41
Robert Ames · Awake and Die #42
Charles Runyon · Object of Lust #43
Dr. Gatskill's Blue Shoes - Paul Conant #44
Murders in Silk - Asa Bordages #45
Take Me As I Am - Darwin Teilhet #46
Blonde Bait - Stephen Marlowe #47
The Fifth Grave - Jonathan Latimer #48
Off Duty - Andrew Coburn #49
Any Man's Girl - Basil Heatter #50

Stark House Press
1315 H Street, Eureka, CA 95501 (707) 498-3135
griffinskye3@sbcglobal.net www.starkhousepress.com
Available from your local bookstore or direct from the publisher

www.ingramcontent.com/pod-product-compliance
Lightning Source LLC
LaVergne TN
LVHW010202070526
838199LV00062B/4461